"Okay?"

Caio's breath near her ear made Ana's heart rate pick up. If she turned her head to the other side they'd be face-to-face. Closer than they'd ever been. He hadn't even kissed her on their wedding day, apart from a perfunctory peck on the mouth at the priest's nudging. And yet it had burned. She nodded. "Fine."

She could sense that he was resting his weight on one arm so as not to crush her to the seat, but Ana felt a pulse throb between her legs and a skewering sensation of need.

She'd fought the desire she'd felt for this man for so long but now it felt as if it was breaking loose. Like a swollen river bursting its banks. She wanted to be crushed under this man. She wanted to feel all of that lean and steely strength around her. *In her.*

She bit her lip. *This* was why she'd booked a flight out of Rio de Janeiro as soon as she could. Her control around this man felt as if it had been fraying for a long time...

Irish author **Abby Green** ended a very glamorous career in film and TV—which really consisted of a lot of standing in the rain outside actors' trailers—to pursue her love of romance. After she'd bombarded Harlequin with manuscripts, they kindly accepted one, and an author was born. She lives in Dublin, Ireland, and loves any excuse for distraction. Visit abby-green.com or email abbygreenauthor@gmail.com.

Books by Abby Green

Harlequin Presents

The Greek's Unknown Bride
Bound by Her Shocking Secret

Hot Summer Nights with a Billionaire

The Flaw in His Red-Hot Revenge

The Marchetti Dynasty

The Maid's Best Kept Secret
The Innocent Behind the Scandal
Bride Behind the Desert Veil

Rival Spanish Brothers

Confessions of a Pregnant Cinderella
Redeemed by His Stolen Bride

Visit the Author Profile page
at Harlequin.com for more titles.

Abby Green

—

THEIR ONE-NIGHT RIO REUNION

Recycling programs
for this product may
not exist in your area.

ISBN-13: 978-1-335-56951-6

Their One-Night Rio Reunion

Copyright © 2022 by Abby Green

All rights reserved. No part of this book may be used or reproduced in
any manner whatsoever without written permission except in the case of
brief quotations embodied in critical articles and reviews.

This is a work of fiction. Names, characters, places and incidents
are either the product of the author's imagination or are used fictitiously.
Any resemblance to actual persons, living or dead, businesses,
companies, events or locales is entirely coincidental.

This edition published by arrangement with Harlequin Books S.A.

For questions and comments about the quality of this book,
please contact us at CustomerService@Harlequin.com.

Harlequin Enterprises ULC
22 Adelaide St. West, 41st Floor
Toronto, Ontario M5H 4E3, Canada
www.Harlequin.com

Printed in U.S.A.

THEIR ONE-NIGHT RIO REUNION

I'd like to dedicate this to Margaret. For forty-one years, most of my life, she has been woven into the fabric of my existence like no one else. She has taught me, guided me, nurtured me, loved me like her own and brought me into her family like a fierce mama bear. She has brought me immense joy and happiness, and none of this would have been half as much fun or as satisfying without her. Thank you, and I love you.

PROLOGUE

A year ago, Cristo Redentor Church, Rio de Janeiro

ANA DIAZ WAS late to her own wedding. Which was entirely to be expected for a normal wedding. But this wasn't a normal wedding. This was an arranged marriage between two of Brazil's elite families.

She was the pawn in a deal between her media mogul father, Rodolfo Diaz, and billionaire tech entrepreneur Caio Salazar. His full name was Caio Salazar de Barros, but he had turned his back on his family fortune and dynasty some years before and struck out on his own, building his own empire.

However, his association and name, even without 'de Barros', was still very potent currency. Hence the marriage match. Her father needed Caio Salazar for a business deal and Salazar needed a wife, because apparently he was under pressure to project a more settled and conservative image in order to expand his business into Europe and globally.

Ana could understand why—he had cultivated quite the reputation as a playboy. Always staying within the bounds of respectability—just—but leaving no one in any doubt that he was—according to breathless accounts in the gossip columns—a masterful lover of beautiful women, while also enjoying all the trappings that came with unimaginable wealth and success.

Ana could appreciate that that kind of reputation would only take one so far on a global stage. Two things had persuaded her to agree to the marriage. One, she'd manage to secure her beloved younger brother's future, and two, the marriage was to last only for one year.

Clearly that was all the time Salazar could bear to indulge in putting forward a less hedonistic persona.

The prenuptial agreement had stated that she would be required to attend social events with her husband, helping to promote his desired re-branding as a reformed married man. Ana was to do everything to make their union believable by appearing devoted. Connected. *In public.*

Behind closed doors, however, she would

not be expected to keep up the act. She'd been assured of her own private rooms and space. Days off when not required for public duties.

The only ambiguity had been the omission of anything specific about marital relations *in the bedroom*. Her heart palpitated at that thought and a cold sweat broke out over her skin. Not because she feared the prospect or didn't find her fiancé attractive. Quite the opposite.

From the moment she'd laid eyes on Caio Salazar in her father's house, when he'd first come to discuss business some weeks ago, he'd branded himself onto her consciousness in a way that was seriously disturbing.

Tall and dark, with a leanly muscular build, he was undeniably handsome. His thick dark hair was kept short, but long enough to frame a hard-boned face. Dark brows lay over deep-set eyes and an aquiline nose that more than hinted at his impeccable lineage, all the way back to the Portuguese *conquistadores* of Brazil. His mouth was sculpted and firm. Sensual. His jaw was hard and more often stubbled than not. His eyes were dark. He oozed an arrogant potent sexuality that made his playboy reputation only too easy to believe.

She'd watched him covertly when he'd come to meet with her father in a series of secret meetings, arriving on each occasion without an entourage—unheard of in the company her father usually kept. Uncoiling his tall, lean body from a low-slung sports car, wearing faded jeans and short-sleeved polo shirts, he'd clearly felt no obligation to adhere to formality, which had intrigued and thrilled Ana in equal measure. It was very seldom she saw anyone exhibit such loucheness around her father.

She'd been surprised to find herself reacting to him so forcefully. She'd never imagined she'd find such an obviously handsome playboy type attractive—especially when he was a product of the same very privileged and cynical world as all of the men she'd grown up with: her father and older brothers.

Her younger brother, Francisco, was different. Vastly different. Which was why she loved him so much. Enough to enter into an arranged marriage.

But something about Caio Salazar had called to her before she could deny it or stop it. On a very deep, base level, where she hid all her insecurities around her inexperience with men. Or, more accurately, her *zero* experience.

Growing up in a house surrounded by men had led to Ana hiding herself away, disguising her femininity, fading into the background. Without a mother and sisters, she'd always felt like an outsider among her peers in school—left out of some essential feminine mystery she should understand but didn't. Together with her natural introversion, it was the reason why she was still untouched at the age of twenty-two, on the verge of walking down the aisle to meet her husband, who might or might not expect to demand his conjugal rights.

She knew that if Caio Salazar did demand his conjugal rights it would be purely because it was a formality, maybe even a legal necessity, so she couldn't back out of the marriage prematurely. *Not* because he would want to. Because she wasn't remotely his type. He favoured tall, leggy models who resembled racehorses, not women of average height, with unfashionable curves and a severe lack of sense of style.

As if hearing her thoughts, her father, who had been on his cell-phone all this time, finally finished his conversation and joined her in the vestibule of the church.

His cold dark gaze, even today, when he was giving her away, raked her up and down. 'You look like an old maid in that dress. Do you want Salazar to decide he's making a huge mistake?'

Ana fought down the anger and the heat of self-consciousness. She'd deliberately chosen this dress because it effectively covered her from neck to toe and shoulder to wrist. She'd wanted to send out a strong signal that she was not to be considered a sexual pawn as well as a marriage pawn. Because right now the thing she feared most was the humiliation of her husband-to-be's realisation that she was as predictably and helplessly in his thrall as every other woman on the planet. That she wanted him with a burning desire that shocked her as much as it dismayed her.

The one meaningful interaction she'd had with Salazar up to now—a mere four weeks ago—flashed into her head. Her father had hauled her in front of the man and presented her like a brood mare to be inspected. Salazar hadn't even looked at her father when he'd said curtly, 'Leave us.'

If it had been another situation Ana might have appreciated the comical sight of Rodolfo Diaz being ordered out of his own reception room. But her father was nothing if not cunning and smart, and he'd known that Salazar agreeing to take his troublesome only daughter off his hands was too good a prospect to mess up, so he'd swallowed his outrage and left them.

Ana had been incandescent with rage at the thought that she was going to be passed from father to husband like a medieval chattel. But Caio Salazar had just looked at her for a long, unnerving moment before saying, 'Do you want to see the world, Ana? Because that is what I'm offering you. I'm taking my company global. All I need is a wife who will stand by my side, unobtrusive and complementary, for one year.'

A little stunned at his candour, and at the fact that he wasn't trying to flirt to persuade her, Ana had taken a moment to gather her wits and push down the residual anger—and, surprisingly, the dart of hurt that she didn't merit even the most rudimentary charm offensive from a renowned playboy.

She'd been terrified he'd notice how being in such close proximity to him was affecting her, and she'd responded tartly, 'Blow-up dolls are very sophisticated these days. You might save yourself a lot of time and money by procuring one for your convenient marriage.'

His dark eyes had flashed at that. The evidence that she'd managed to surprise him had been a small comfort.

He'd drawled, 'Ah, but a blow-up doll hasn't been brought up to navigate the upper echelons of society the way you have, Ana. Everyone wants something…so what is it that you want, or need, that would make this arrangement more…palatable?'

And that was why she was doing this.

For her little brother and ultimately—she couldn't deny it—for herself. For her own freedom.

Ana looked at her father now and bit out, 'If you delay us any longer it won't be because of *me* that Salazar decides to renege on this deal.'

Her father scowled, but nodded to the attendant, who sent a signal to someone, and Ana heard Mendelssohn's "Wedding March" start. She steeled herself as the doors opened and looked down the long aisle to where the tall figure of the man she was about to marry stood. A total stranger, and yet one who had already got under her skin in a way that was seriously disturbing.

CHAPTER ONE

Today, Rio de Janeiro

'MR SALAZAR?'

Caio Salazar turned around to see his solicitor putting some papers down on the wide oak table with little pointed stickers indicating where to sign.

He held out a pen. 'These are the final signatures required for your divorce papers.'

Divorce. Caio Salazar took the pen and sat down.

He had never intended to get married. It hadn't been part of his plans. Not after witnessing his parents' toxic mess of a marriage. He was lucky. He had older brothers who had borne the burden of inheriting the legendary Salazar de Barros wealth and industry, leaving Caio free to strike out on his own and unshackle himself from the yoke of his family, losing 'de Barros' en route.

The success of his self-made business had put paid to any rumours that he wouldn't survive without his family's help. He'd not only survived, he'd become one of Brazil's top net worth individuals, rivalling his own family's dominance single-handedly, leaving him free to live an independent life, beholden to none.

He'd made the most of it at first—cultivating quite the reputation as a playboy rebel, cutting a swathe through Brazil's legendary nightlife and most beautiful women, which had been fun but admittedly had had more to do with irritating his old man than sating his own appetites.

In truth, that life had begun to lose its appeal some time ago. Caio had felt increasingly as if he was going through the motions, living down to a reputation he'd created that no longer served him or amused him.

When his forays into Europe and North America had started falling flat, among rumours that his reputation was too volatile, Caio had realised he was in danger of ruining everything he'd built up. And there were plenty of people waiting to see him take a very public fall from grace.

He wouldn't give them the satisfaction and he wasn't that self-destructive. And so he'd considered the unthinkable—the fastest route to turning his reputation around—a solid marriage to a suitable woman.

Which was why, almost a year ago to the day, he'd married the daughter of one of Rio de Janeiro's most prominent families, taking everyone by surprise.

The marriage had been a serendipitous by-product of a deal with Rodolfo Diaz. The media mogul had a daughter he'd wanted to see married off and Caio had needed a wife. The fact that she came from a suitable background and a similar lineage to Caio had been a bonus. It would make the marriage look even more authentic.

However, Caio had only agreed to think about the union once he'd met with Ana Diaz. Their first meeting hadn't been auspicious. An unfashionably long veil of dark hair had obscured her features and loose clothes had drowned any view of her body. Of average height, she hadn't made much of an impression.

But then her father had taken her chin in his fingers and tipped her face up, and her hair had fallen back to reveal a pretty heart-shaped face, pale, with dark arching brows. Her soft mouth had been set in a mutinous line. Her dark brown eyes had flashed with defiance as her father had spoken to Caio, and she'd pulled away from her father and said angrily, 'I'm not a chattel to be passed around between men.'

In that moment, bristling with tension between father and daughter, Caio had recognised that there was a very real danger that she would provoke her father to violence. He'd smelled it like a metallic tang in the air. He'd known it because he'd smelled it before.

It had impacted him right in his gut, even though she was a complete stranger.

Before he'd had time to analyse his reaction, he'd decided that he would marry her. He'd asked her father to leave them alone to discuss it, and she'd turned that barely concealed fury on him.

To Caio's surprise, even though the woman had been as non-descript as a student, something had pulsed to life in his blood. He'd told himself it was just confirmation that he was making the right decision to save his reputation and move his business forward.

He couldn't have contemplated a marriage of convenience with one of his lovers. That would have spelled disaster and drama. No, marrying a total stranger—albeit one from the right family and background—would be perfect. When they divorced she would be a very rich woman. No harm, no foul.

He'd assured himself that it had nothing to

do with the protective instinct aroused within him when he'd sensed the violence in the air from her father. Or the disturbing physical reaction that he'd dismissed as an aberration as soon as it had happened.

And so, just over a year ago, their wedding had been discreet and conducted with little fanfare. It had caused a flurry of interest at first, but that had died down quickly. After all, strategic marriages between the offspring of Brazil's wealthiest families happened all the time.

And today, the divorce was an equally understated affair.

In many regards the marriage had been a complete success. Ana had travelled the world with him as he'd taken his company global, opening offices in New York, London and Bangkok. With a wife by his side, he'd been accepted among the business community and society without question, because he was no longer a playboy threatening to leave a storm of headlines in his wake as he bedded his way through Europe and North America.

In fact, much to Caio's surprise, he'd found that he'd been singularly *un*-enticed by any of the women who had made it very clear that they were available. He'd discovered that having a wife was no deterrent in that regard.

Caio looked across the room at the back of the woman who stood in front of one of the floor-to-ceiling windows that showcased a jaw-dropping view of the financial district of Rio de Janeiro, early-morning sunlight making the tall buildings sparkle and shine.

His wife no longer had unfashionably long hair. Now it was cut much shorter, into a bob that brushed her shoulders and framed her face. A face that he hadn't fully appreciated when they'd first met. A face that had revealed its beauty in such a way as to mock Caio daily for having first assumed she was average.

She wore a little make-up now, expertly applied, highlighting dark, long-lashed brown eyes framed by naturally arching brows. Her light olive skin was flawless. Her nose had a slightly patrician bump. But it was her mouth that he'd grown more and more fixated by: soft and naturally pouting, it sometimes gave her an air of intense vulnerability and sometimes, more recently and disturbingly, an air of something much closer to sultry, almost provocative.

The shapeless clothes she'd favoured when they'd first met were long gone. Today she wore a designer slim-fitting black trouser suit paired with a grey silk shirt and black high heels, drawing attention to her slender ankles.

Discreet jewellery. Even in heels, she was still a full head shorter than him.

A low cough alerted him to the fact that his solicitor was still waiting for him to sign the papers.

What the hell was wrong with him?

This marriage had always been destined to end today, and Caio had achieved exactly what he'd set out to achieve a year ago. Ignoring the knot of resistance in his gut, Caio signed the papers and handed the pen back to his solicitor.

Ana Diaz Salazar heard the sound of a pen moving over paper behind her. Her husband… signing their divorce papers. Next, it would be her turn. So why wasn't she more impatient to get this divorce signed, sealed and delivered?

She'd stood in this very same spot just over a year ago, when she'd come here to sign the prenuptial agreement. Then, as now, she fancied that she could almost see all the way to where the early-morning surf would be foaming up onto the famous Copacabana beach.

She longed to be there now. It was her favourite time to be on the beach—early, before it became packed with fellow Cariocas. Or, better yet, to be there with her beloved younger brother Francisco. Except he was many thousands of miles away, in Europe. Where she'd be heading too, this afternoon, on a one-way plane ticket, as a newly divorced millionairess—thanks to the very generous settlement from her husband. A settlement that would have been even larger if she hadn't insisted that she didn't feel entitled to the money.

She waited for a feeling of excitement to grip her at the thought of flying to Europe with enough funds to start a new life but, much to her irritation, any sense of excitement was tempered with frustration. Regret. Unfinished business. *Unrequited desire*, whispered a sly voice in her ear.

She slammed a lid on that incendiary notion. She'd come far too close to humiliating herself, trying to get her husband to notice her in recent weeks, as if in desperation as their divorce date had come closer. The inconvenient desire she'd felt for him at the start of their marriage had only grown stronger, as if to mock her daily. Like a thorn under her skin. A constant reminder that she was weak.

Thank God they were divorcing today and she would be able to put some distance between them with her dignity more or less intact. He would never know how much she wanted him. Because he'd never really noticed her.

'Mrs Salazar? We're ready for you to sign.'

Ana tensed. *Mrs Salazar*. Not for much longer. She would be Ana Diaz again after this. She could feel her husband's eyes on her back. But was he even really her husband if they hadn't consummated their marriage? They'd lived together, yes, and they'd travelled—*a lot*—and had attended events as husband and wife, but apart from that contact had been minimal.

Business associates probably spent more time together. Knew each other more intimately. Except…she did feel as if she knew her husband intimately. On a level that was very secret, where she'd watched him avidly, discovering that he was a man far different from the one she'd first judged him to be.

Caio had become too intriguing for Ana's liking and when intrigue was packaged with physical attraction… Her feelings for him now added up to something she didn't even want to articulate.

'Ana?'

His deep voice cut through the chatter in her head and made the tangle in her gut knot even tighter. She took a deep breath and turned around, steeling herself for her husband's effect on her.

But even steeling herself didn't work. Her blood leapt and her pulse-rate tripled. She worried that his image would be permanently etched onto her brain. And his dark eyes that weren't completely dark. They had golden flecks up close that made them look molten. She knew because she'd seen them turn molten one night...

They'd moved around so much in the past year that it had become normal for her to feel a little disorientated when she woke at night in a new place—a hotel suite or one of Caio's residences. That particular night she'd been walking sleepily back into her bedroom after getting a glass of water and a sound had made her look up. She'd registered too late that she hadn't returned to her room. It was Caio's, and he'd been emerging from a cloud of steam, obviously having just taken a shower in the bathroom.

The incendiary sight before her had glued her feet to the spot. He had been entirely naked. Drying his hair roughly with a small towel. Dark olive skin still damp. Gleaming.

In that moment Ana had understood why sculptors created works of art dedicated to the male form. His chest was a hard and broad expanse, covered in a light smattering of dark hair, muscles bunching and moving as he'd dried his hair. A dark line of hair dissected the well-defined six-pack of his abdomen before disappearing into the thicket of hair that cradled the very essence of his masculinity. Lean hips and powerful thighs. Long legs.

But she hadn't been able to take her eyes off that most potent part of him. Even at rest it had been impressive.

A heavy, tugging ache between her legs had made her press her thighs together, as if she could contain the longing. And then the hand holding the small towel had dropped, obscuring her vision. Only then had she been able to break out of her trance and her stricken gaze had met his. And that was when she'd noticed for the first time how his eyes could look... molten. Not just dark and frustratingly unreadable, as she'd often told herself, but actually...hot. Hotter than the sun.

She'd fled.

'Ana?'

His voice jerked her out of the past and back into the present. Those dark brows were drawn together now. That sensual mouth was tight. She would have expected him to be more relaxed. He was getting rid of the wife he'd married only to further his business interests.

He could go out now and take any number of beautiful women to bed and slake his lust—because she knew he hadn't taken any lovers during their marriage. He'd respected their sham marriage vows. And that had only confused her even more.

She blinked. 'Yes, I'm ready.'

She dragged her gaze away from his and looked down at the table, where her solicitor was pointing to the dotted line and handing her a pen, saying, 'The last signature, Mrs Salazar. This will complete the paperwork.'

Ana took the pen. It felt unbearably heavy. She bent down and noticed that her hand was trembling. Angry with herself for reacting like this to an event that she'd anticipated since the day she'd agreed to marry this man, she scrawled her name and the pen dropped out of her nerveless fingers.

Done.

The marriage of convenience she'd entered into with the utmost reluctance was now over and it hadn't been what she'd expected it to be at all. It had been…something else entirely…

CHAPTER TWO

CAIO WATCHED AS Ana straightened from signing her name. She looked…agitated. Biting her lip. His insides twisted with helpless reaction. He tensed against it and reminded himself that the sooner she was gone, the better. His reaction to her was just a build-up of sexual frustration after a year of celibacy.

But no other woman has interested you, pointed out a mocking voice.

Caio ignored it.

He'd got what he needed out of the mutually beneficial arrangement and it was time to move on. He'd go out tonight, arrange to meet one of his ex-lovers who'd made it very clear throughout the last year that she was available if he so desired…

Yet right now it was hard even to recall what she looked like. And the thought of going through the charade of wining and dining and indulging in inane conversation was suddenly very unappealing.

Slightly disgusted with himself, Caio wondered if a year of domesticity—even if it had been a charade—had somehow rewired his brain?

You could have seduced Ana, taunted another voice.

Caio's mouth firmed into a tight line. Seducing her had not been an option. She was a virgin, and she'd been so terrified on their wedding night that he would force her to sleep with him that she'd tried to run away. He'd assured her that he wouldn't touch her during their marriage, because he didn't sleep with innocents.

And he still didn't.

Time to move on.

The chief legal advisor looked first at Ana and then at Caio. She said, 'Once the decree is signed off by the court, the divorce will be final. That will happen within the next twenty-four hours. But essentially, as of this moment, you can consider yourselves divorced.'

Ana swallowed past the obstruction that had appeared out of nowhere in her throat. She forced herself to say, 'Thank you.'

The legal advisor cracked a small smile.

'I just wish every divorce was as amicable and respectful as yours—it would make life a lot easier.'

Ana's face grew hot, and she avoided Caio's eye. It was pretty much common knowledge that her marriage to Caio Salazar had been one borne out of a business arrangement between Caio and her father, even if Caio *had* made sure the final decision was hers.

The legal team were starting to file out of the office now, talking in low voices, and the sound of their chatter broke Ana out of her reverie. She reached for her bag on the table and Caio walked over to join her. All the tiny hairs on her body vibrated with awareness. She didn't like the wrenching sensation in her gut. She gritted her jaw. The sooner she was out of his disturbing orbit the better.

'My driver is outside to take us home.'

Home. Ana wanted to reject the notion that Caio's Rio de Janeiro penthouse apartment had been a home to her, but in fact it had become more of a home than her own had ever been, and the thought of never seeing it again made her feel acutely vulnerable.

She shook her head. 'Thanks, but my flight to Europe leaves in a few hours. I'm going to go straight to the airport.' She forced down a dart of inexplicable guilt and looked at him.

'It's not as if we need to pretend any more, do we?'

He looked at her intently. A muscle ticked in his jaw. She could see the golden flecks in his eyes so clearly now, and wondered why it had taken her so long to notice them. Maybe because she'd avoided looking at him directly for a long time. Scared of his effect on her. And maybe because for many weeks after they'd married she'd still been crippled by the lingering humiliation of her father completely exposing her.

When he'd found out that she'd agreed to the marriage, Rodolfo Diaz had boomed in his loud voice, 'Excellent! And let me assure you that you are getting a wife not only of impeccable breeding but also one who still has her virtue intact. How many twenty-two-year-olds can claim that in this day and age?'

Ana still burned at the excoriating memory a year later. She'd wanted alternately to throttle her father and to disappear about a thousand feet under the earth. But Caio hadn't appeared shocked. He hadn't been remotely interested in whether or not Ana was innocent, as she'd found out on her wedding night. Just to compound her humiliation.

Eventually Caio responded, breaking Ana

out of her painful reminiscences. 'What's your plan when you get to Europe?'

Ana said, 'I've rented an apartment near Francisco for six months. I can figure out where to go from there. I've arranged for my things to be put in storage until I know where I'll be long-term.'

Caio's expression was impossible to read. Even now. He clearly couldn't care less that she was leaving—he was just being polite, making it appear as if her imminent departure wasn't something he'd been waiting for for weeks. It made something rebellious and volatile bubble up inside her—a need to see that polite façade crack.

But before Ana could say something—anything to try and provoke some last reaction—there was a sharp rap on the door, and they both looked around to see Caio's chief of security, Tomás, who organised the discreet security detail that followed them both daily. He looked serious, and apologised for interrupting so precipitately.

Tomás acknowledged Ana and then addressed Caio. 'Mr Salazar, we have a situation and it's serious.'

'What is it?' Caio's voice was sharp.

The man answered, 'It's a kidnap threat, and it's very credible. They're here, in the city right now, highly organised and motivated. We need to extract you and Mrs Salazar straight away and remove you to a secure location.'

Ana felt that now wasn't the time to point out that technically she was no longer Mrs Salazar. She wasn't overly shocked at this news. Growing up as a Diaz, daughter to one of Brazil's wealthiest businessmen, she had never known what it was to live without the threat of violence or kidnap. Security had been a constant feature of her life, and in many ways she'd grown used to it.

She took a step forward, feeling slightly panicky that there might be a delay in putting Rio de Janeiro and Caio and all the disturbing things he made her feel, behind her. That was more of a threat.

'I'm due to fly to Europe this afternoon— surely I'll be safe there?'

Tomás looked at her, and he was grimmer than she'd ever seen him. 'Mrs Salazar, we have it on good authority that two of the kidnappers are on your flight and have plans to snatch you once you're through Customs in Amsterdam.'

Ana gulped.

Tomás looked at Caio. 'And they are planning a simultaneous operation with you here, Mr Salazar. They are going to substitute your driver with one of theirs, so that they can take you to a location and inform you of the kidnap of your wife and lay out their demands. They're not planning on freeing you until their demands are met.'

A cold finger traced down Ana's spine at the thought of Caio being put in danger.

The man continued. 'They've been operating for some time, and they're wanted by every security agency in the world. They're the same gang who kidnapped the daughter of Federico Falluci in Italy and got a massive ransom.'

Ana went even colder. She'd heard about that. The little girl hadn't spoken for months afterwards.

'This is the first time they've managed to track the gang down and discover who they're targeting next.'

Ana shook her head. 'But we're divorced... or as good as...what worth have I to them?'

'They will have been observing you for months by now. They only go after targets they know will do whatever it takes to retrieve the victim and pay the ransom.'

Before Ana could respond to that, Caio addressed Tomás, 'So what's the plan?'

Ana turned to face him. 'What's the plan? The plan is that I go to Europe today. They've

targeted the wrong people!' The thought of
Caio caring enough to bankrupt himself to
save her was almost laughable, except Ana
didn't feel like laughing.

The security man was shaking his head.
'I'm afraid that's not possible, Mrs Salazar.
The special security forces are involved now.
This is bigger than you or us. We have organised a safe location for you both to go to, but
you need to leave immediately. Staff have prepared essential items for you.'

Ana looked at the man. 'Go where? For how
long?'

'I'm afraid I can't tell you that. You'll find
out when you get there. As for how long? At
least twenty-four hours. That's the window of
time we have to catch this gang, before they
realise they're being watched.'

Her head reeling at this abrupt turn of
events, Ana repeated faintly, 'Twenty-four
hours…?'

CHAPTER THREE

EVERYTHING BECAME A blur of activity after that. Ana and Caio were taken down to the basement of the building in a staff elevator and put into the back of a non-descript, shabby SUV with blacked-out windows. They were instructed to lie down until told otherwise and Ana complied, suddenly more frightened than she'd ever been by the sheer level of security that had sprung up around them. Some of the men were wearing full protection gear and holding massive guns.

She lay down on the back seat, turning her head to one side, and Caio had no option but to cover her body with his. Far from getting away from him, she was now closer to him than she'd ever been.

The vehicle started to move—up a ramp and presumably out onto a side street.

She was burningly aware of Caio's body over hers. Her bottom was cupped by his hard thighs and that memory of his naked image filled her mind.

She gritted her jaw. *Not helping*.

His hands were beside hers on the seat, laughably bigger than hers. His scent filled her nostrils, heady and masculine. She could feel the heat of his body through his clothes.

He generally erred on the side of being casual, working in an industry that wasn't renowned for conforming at the best of times, but today she'd been surprised to see him wearing a dark three-piece suit. A dark blue tie.

The only other time she could recall him wearing a three-piece suit—apart from their wedding—had been the day she'd signed the prenuptial agreement. It had completely intimidated her the first time around. The suit had made him look remote and like a stranger. But today... All she'd been able to see was the man under the suit. A man full of many more contradictions that she could have ever imagined. A man she'd come to respect.

And more.

The suit was a reminder that he was one of the richest self-made men in Brazil. After ostracising himself from his family and rejecting any inheritance he was due a long time ago, he'd sold his first start-up to one of the big Silicon Valley companies for many millions at the tender age of twenty-four. And since then he'd only become more successful. Everything he touched turned to gold.

Ana had always wondered about why he'd turned his back on his family, but whenever she'd broached the subject Caio had firmly diverted the conversation. Fair enough. She didn't particularly relish discussions about her family either. They had that much in common.

'Okay?'

Caio's breath near her ear made Ana's heart-rate pick up. If she turned her head to the other side they'd be face to face. Closer than they'd ever been. He hadn't even kissed her on their wedding day, apart from a perfunctory peck on the mouth at the priest's nudging. And yet it had burned.

She nodded. 'Fine.'

She could sense that he was resting his weight on one arm, so as not to crush her to the seat, but Ana felt a pulse throb between her legs and a skewering sensation of need. She'd fought the desire she felt for this man for so long, but now it felt as if it was breaking loose. Like a swollen river bursting its banks. She *wanted* to be crushed under this man. She wanted to feel all that lean and steely strength around her. *In her.*

She bit her lip. *This* was why she'd booked a flight out of Rio de Janeiro as soon as she could. She felt as if her control around this man had been fraying for a long time, and she'd been veering into dangerous territory recently, wanting to provoke a reaction—as if she needed to prove to herself once and for all that he saw her as merely a by-product of a business deal.

A deal that was now going to be prolonged for another twenty-four hours in a secret location...

Tomás's voice came from the front of the vehicle. 'You can sit up now, Mr and Mrs Salazar, it's safe.'

Suddenly Caio's heat and weight were gone. Ana felt ridiculously bereft. She sat up slowly. They seemed to be driving into some kind of small airfield with a hangar nearby.

Tomás said, 'We weren't followed, but we took a circuitous route just in case. The helicopter is waiting here. If we'd taken you from the roof of your building it would have raised suspicions.'

'Won't they be suspicious when we don't come out of the building? When I don't get on the plane later?' Ana pointed out.

Tomás's eyes met Ana's in the mirror.

'There's a plan in place, Mrs Salazar, and that's all I can tell you. You'll find out more if it's successful.'

Ana shivered. *If* it was successful.

As if sensing her sudden trepidation, Caio took her hand. She looked at him, surprised by the contact. 'Nothing will happen to you, I promise,' he said.

Ana swallowed. For a moment she could almost imagine that there'd been something fierce in his voice. But then Caio abruptly let go of her hand, as if aware that he'd transgressed their tacit agreement only to touch in public. For the purposes of a marriage that no longer existed.

The SUV came to a stop and Ana saw the helicopter, its blades circling slowly outside the hangar. Staff waited along with more men in dark clothes with guns.

They were escorted to the helicopter under strict surveillance. She got in first, followed by Caio, and before she could take a breath she was strapped in, headphones on, and they were lifting up into the sky with a little wobble.

Ana gripped her armrests and after a few minutes looked down and saw Rio de Janeiro sprawling along the coast, early-morning sunlight glinting off tall buildings. The slightly misty outline of the famous Cristo Redentor statue dominated the top of the Corcovado mountain, arms outstretched.

Soon they were high above the Atlantic Ocean, leaving the coastline behind, and Ana could see nothing but a vast expanse of dark blue water. After about fifteen minutes the helicopter started circling an area. Ana looked down, and at first she could see nothing. But then she saw it: a tiny jewel of an island, rocky and lushly green, with a wide sandy beach and dense foliage. Waves broke and foamed against the shore. What looked like a sprawling villa sat in the cleared centre, and as they descended she could make out a huge pool set in lush, manicured grounds. There was also a pier, and a yacht bobbing in the water.

It was as if someone had plucked what Ana imagined to be a fantasy island out of her head and planted it here in the middle of the ocean.

They landed on a clear expanse of lawn, not too far from the villa, which Ana could see was artfully camouflaged with lush foliage so that it almost seemed to emerge fully formed from the landscape. Definitely the work of an architect—and a renowned one at that, she guessed.

When they got out, they were met by an efficient woman in a uniform of black trousers and crisp white shirt, saying, 'Welcome to Ilha

Pequena. I'm Estella, the estate manager.' As she walked them to the villa she explained that the kitchen was stocked with enough provisions for a week.

Ana stopped in her tracks. *A week?*

Estella showed them around the open-plan airy villa, with its wide, deeply varnished floorboards. It was decorated with the kind of understated elegance that only serious money could buy, and yet it was also charmingly lived-in. Ana had the sense that, whoever's home this was, it was very much loved and enjoyed, not treated like a museum, in spite of the very expensive art she recognised on the walls.

She spotted bowls for dog food and water in the kitchen. She could imagine a family here…children running in and out of the French doors that opened out from the kitchen/dining area to the lawn…and the image made a dart of longing pierce her gut, exposing her.

She'd told herself long ago that happy families were pure illusion. Maybe for other people who lived simpler lives, but not for people like her. All her tender fantasies had been blasted apart the day her mother had walked out of the family home, abandoning her husband and children, and so Ana had always been very careful not to allow herself to imagine even for a second that she could have something she'd never even experienced.

But in spite of everything she knew, the fantasy persisted, deep inside her, like a stubborn illicit stain. A dream of a happy family like the ones she saw on TV. Or in the movies. Or in books. She'd always loved the image of Tiny Tim and his loving, humble family from *A Christmas Carol*—she'd read that story over and over to her brother Francisco when they were younger.

Ana turned away from the view and castigated herself. *Pathetic.*

They were shown next into a luxurious but obviously lived-in lounge, with huge comfortable couches and armchairs, where a projector was set up, along with a state-of-the-art smart TV and music system. Also on the ground level was another more formal lounge, a library, a study, a gym and a dining room.

Upstairs there were numerous bedrooms, most of them closed off—Ana guessed they belonged to the children—and a master suite.

'These two bedrooms are free for you to use,' Estella said, indicating two rooms on opposite sides of the corridor. She opened the door on the left. 'I put you in here, Mrs Salazar, I hope it'll be sufficient?'

Ana realised that she'd grown so used to

being shown into her own separate room that she didn't even wonder any more what people might think.

That whole side of her marriage with Caio had been handled with discreet efficiency. When not in the apartment in Rio, they'd either been in apartments belonging to him around the world, or hotel suites with enough rooms for people not to know what their sleeping arrangements were.

The door opened into a pretty bedroom suite dressed in cool whites and blues. A vast four-poster bed dominated the room, and there was an en-suite bathroom with rolltop bath. There was a dressing room, and a balcony terrace, overlooking the back gardens. She could see the ocean and hear the waves lapping against the shore. It was more than *sufficient*.

When Ana looked inside the dressing room she was surprised to see the clothes she'd packed for Europe hanging up or folded neatly onto shelves, alongside clothes she'd never seen before. 'But…how?'

Estella said, 'Essential items were picked up for you both from your apartment and sent out with me on the first helicopter trip, along with other supplies. They thought it best to alert you only at the last minute, in case anyone found out about the plan. The other clothes are here for guests' use. Feel free to help yourself to anything that makes you more comfortable.'

Ana balked a little as the full enormity of the operation to get them out of Rio and to this place sank in. She asked, 'Who owns this estate?'

'Luca Fonseca. He was prepared to give you the use of the island as I believe he knows Mr Salazar.'

Ana looked at Caio, who was nodding. 'We go back a bit. He was one of my first investors.'

Estella was continuing, 'The island estate was bought for his wife as a wedding anniversary present some years ago.'

Something twisted inside Ana at this mention of one of Brazil's most famous couples. They were famous not only for being who they were—Serena Fonseca, née DePiero, was the daughter of an infamous and disgraced Italian tycoon—but also because they seemed to be genuinely in love and conducted a very happy private family life with their three children and their extended family.

Fêted and adored by the press, the blonde beauty and her handsome Brazilian husband were rarely spotted, which only added to their allure. And with hideaway private islands like this to escape to, Ana could understand how they stayed under the radar.

Estella was showing Caio into his bedroom across the hall. Similar to Ana's, it differed only in colour scheme, being decorated in shades of dark grey and white, set off beautifully against the same very simple floorboards that ran through the entire villa. Artisanal rugs added softness and pops of colour against the otherwise muted interiors.

Ana followed Caio into his dressing room, to see him indicate to where one of his tuxedoes was hanging up. 'I don't think I'll be needing this.' His tone was dry.

Estella shrugged. 'Best to be prepared for every eventuality. Please, feel free to explore all you want and make yourselves at home. I have to return to Rio de Janeiro.'

'You're not staying?' Ana didn't like the tinge of panic in her voice. But she was nervous of being alone in this idyllic and totally unexpected place with Caio. Especially when her emotions were so close to the surface.

Emotions? Who was she kidding? It was her desire she was afraid of.

The woman shook her head. 'No, unfortunately I have work to do for Mr Fonseca. You'll have everything you need, and your protection team will be keeping watch from security boats stationed around the island for as long as they're needed.'

Ana went back into her bedroom and looked out to sea from her small terrace. Sure enough, she could see a boat on the water, and then another at a distance. She breathed out a shaky breath, wrapping her hands around the terrace railing, and tried to absorb the fact that an hour ago she'd been on the mainland, newly divorced and about to head to the airport to start a new life.

Now what?

CHAPTER FOUR

Caio stood on the terrace outside the open-plan kitchen and watched the helicopter take off, the loud *thwack* of its blades fading as it sped over the ocean back to the mainland. He pulled absently at his tie, feeling constricted. He was still reeling at the speed with which they'd been despatched here.

All he could see in his mind's eye, though, was Ana's huge brown eyes filled with shock. Her face so pale. Not out of fear. Out of shock that she wasn't getting away from Caio fast enough.

He still couldn't believe she'd booked a flight out of Rio that very day. Couldn't she even bear a few more days in his company? It made a mockery of his sense that their relationship had reached a level of *simpatico*. Understanding. Mutual respect. Friendship.

Clearly he'd misread it. Badly.

He heard a sound behind him and turned

around to see Ana. She'd taken off her jacket and the top button of her shirt was undone. She was barefoot, hair a little tousled, as if she'd run a hand through it. He could see the curves of her breasts through the thin material encased in plain white. Lace? Or silk?

His blood quickened and grew hot, but he'd become a master at disguising her effect on him. She was looking at him warily. It made the heat in his blood surge even more.

'You had no inkling of this?' she asked.

He shook his head. 'I can understand their logic in not telling us till the last moment, in case we accidentally tipped the kidnappers off that we knew.'

'Do you think they'll get them?'

'My security firm is the same one used by Luca Fonseca—that's presumably how he was approached about using his island. And considering his level of zeal when it comes to protecting his family, together with the involvement of the special forces, if they can't catch them then I don't know who can.' He couldn't help adding with a slight bite to his voice, 'Don't worry, I'll have my assistant book you on the next available flight to Europe as soon as we get back to Rio. I know you're eager to leave.'

A flare of pink appeared in Ana's cheeks.

She lifted her chin. 'I would have thought you'd be pleased to get your life back. You only married me for a business deal.'

'You married me to secure your brother's freedom and future, as well as your own,' Caio reminded her. 'So you got something out of it too.'

She immediately looked chastened. 'Yes, I did get something out of it—and so did Francisco. We're both grateful for that.'

He clenched his jaw. 'I didn't mention that to ask for your gratitude.'

'I know. And you have treated me with the utmost respect. What could have been a nightmare scenario was...*not*.'

'You mean the bit where you thought I was going to demand my conjugal rights on our wedding night?' He still smarted to think that she'd been so averse to the idea of sleeping with her husband that she'd tried to run away.

Ana's cheeks flushed. 'We hadn't covered that in the prenuptial agreement. I didn't know you... I didn't know what to expect. What *you* would expect.'

She bit her lip, as if to stop more words spilling out. Caio wanted to know what she was holding back but she stayed silent.

He sighed. 'I can't blame you, after meeting your father. It was only natural you'd fear that I was similar.'

'I wasn't scared of you.'

Caio looked at Ana and saw the defiant set of her chin. It made his mouth want to quirk. He could recall only too easily how pale she'd been that night, when he'd found her trying to open a staff entrance door to the apartment. She'd changed out of her wedding dress and had been dressed in jeans and a loose top. Her hair, long and silky, had been tumbling over her shoulders and down her back...

He folded his arms and regarded her now. 'Where were you even planning on going?'

Caio hadn't asked her that question at the time. Why now?

Ana prickled self-consciously under his gaze. It reminded her too much of the sense of exposure she'd felt when she'd stood beside him on their wedding day in her very plain, long white dress overlaid with lace. The dress that had made her look *'like an old maid'*, as her father had stated so memorably.

She'd thought it was a good idea, sending a strong signal to Caio not to view her as anything but a convenient wife, but standing beside him she'd felt hideously frumpy and out of date.

The indiscreet whisperings of the stylist to the hair and make-up team hired to get her ready had come back to haunt her.

'This man is Brazil's sexiest playboy...is she deliberately trying to turn him off?'

Ana had fought the urge to turn around and inform the woman that that was her plan precisely.

She'd always told herself she didn't care what people thought, but when they'd arrived at the church and everyone had turned to look at her, including Caio, she'd never felt more exposed. She'd felt as if everyone was judging her and finding her lacking. She'd never been more acutely aware of the fact that not even her own mother had found her lovable enough to stay.

Those few steps down the aisle had been the longest of her life, but she'd found to her surprise that Caio's gaze had searched for hers and held it the whole way down. As if he was silently commanding her to think only of him and nothing else. And for that moment she *had* thought of nothing else.

But then, up close, he'd been so intimidating—resplendent in a steel-grey morning suit, clean-shaven, hair swept back—and all her self-consciousness had surged back. She'd burned with embarrassment. And awareness.

By the time they'd returned to Caio's apartment that evening Ana had been a bag of jangling nerves, exhausted after a long day of meeting more people than she'd met in her lifetime. Seriously wondering if she'd made a huge mistake.

She really hadn't known what Caio would expect after her stunt with the wedding dress, and she'd imagined him appearing in her bedroom, demanding to consummate their marriage. She'd even thought that it might be a legal requirement. She'd imagined the humiliation of his finding out that she really *was* a virgin. That her father hadn't lied.

Not to mention the humiliation that she wanted him.

So…she'd panicked.

She'd changed and packed and found the staff entrance to the apartment. And then Caio had appeared behind her, divested of his wedding waistcoat and tie, top button of his shirt open.

'Ana? Where the hell are you going?'

She'd turned around, gripping her small case. She'd felt very young and very foolish. And vulnerable.

Caio's hands had been on his hips, effortlessly drawing attention to the leanness of his waist. She'd swallowed painfully before saying, 'I don't know what you're expecting, but I won't sleep with you.'

That dark, impenetrable gaze had swept up and down, humiliating her even further, because she had known exactly how she must look while Caio had oozed male sophistication. And then she'd realised in that moment, with bone-chilling horror, that she'd got it all wrong. This was not a man who would lower himself to take an unwilling wife. He would have sophisticated, experienced mistresses for his needs.

As if reading her mind, he'd said coolly, 'I don't know what *you* are expecting, but I don't sleep with virgins, Ana. You're quite safe from me, I assure you. This marriage will not extend to the bedroom. It's a business agreement, for one year, as stipulated in the prenuptial agreement.'

He'd reached for the door then, and opened it onto a plain corridor, bright with harsh emergency lighting and leading to stairs down to the lower levels.

'By all means, leave if you want to. I'm no gaoler. But if you do, I can't promise that your father will keep to his end of the agreement and allow your brother to pursue his art studies in Europe.'

Drowning in embarrassment, Ana had remembered why she'd married Caio in the first place. For her brother. So he could get away from their family's toxic environment and follow his dreams.

She'd used her hair to try and hide her burning face as much as possible. 'I'm not going anywhere.'

Caio had simply shut the door again and said, 'Goodnight, then, Ana. Sleep well.'

He'd walked back into the apartment and Ana had battled with wanting the ground to open up and swallow her whole and the gut-punching realisation that he didn't want her, and how that felt like a jagged piece of glass between her ribs.

And now, a year on from that night, one thing was crystal-clear: she needn't have worried about unwanted or wanted advances from her husband, because he wouldn't have touched her if she'd begged him to.

'Ana?' Caio prompted, frowning.

Ana struggled to recall what he'd asked. *'Where were you even planning on going?'*

She shook her head. 'It doesn't matter now.' She needed to escape from that incisive gaze. As lightly as she could, she said, 'I think I'll explore a little, and change into something more comfortable.'

'I'll see what provisions we have and prepare some lunch.'

'Don't worry about me,' Ana said quickly. 'I can look after myself.'

Caio unfolded his arms and slipped the shades resting on his head down to cover his eyes. 'Suit yourself.'

He turned and walked back inside the villa.

CHAPTER FIVE

IMMEDIATELY ANA FELT churlish and childish. It had taken the full year for her to emerge from her shell and feel she could stand with this man in public and not stick out like a sore thumb. But right now she felt as gauche as she had on their wedding day.

She cursed herself. It was going to be a very long twenty-four hours. But surely with a vast villa and sprawling grounds between them they could keep their distance?

Ana made her way down to the lawn, past the vast pool, its surface barely rippling in the light breeze, towards the beach.

She told herself she was being paranoid to think for a second that Caio cared if she ate with him or not. No doubt, in his mind, this whole security threat was just an unfortunate speed bump on the road to getting his life back to normal. Ana could well imagine the legion of beautiful women lining up, waiting to entice Brazil's hottest newly minted bachelor back into their beds. He'd undoubtedly already lined up a woman to celebrate his first night of freedom with—except now he was stuck here.

Ana reached the beach. Wide, pristine, empty. The Atlantic Ocean was calm today, but she could imagine that it would be breathtaking on a stormy day, lashing the beach and swirling around the island.

But her mind wasn't on the view. It was on Caio. He'd seemed surprised that she was insisting on leaving Rio today. And almost... Ana shook her head. No way had he been *hurt*. He didn't care for her. But then, a little voice pointed out, he didn't *not* care for her.

She sat down on the sand, under the shade of a palm tree. The sun was merciless even at mid-morning at this latitude.

A memory resurfaced. She'd been married to Caio for about two months, and they'd been in Bangkok for the launch of Caio's South East Asian office, staying in a stunning penthouse hotel suite with views over the Chao Phraya river as it snaked its way through the teeming Asian city.

The sights, sounds, smells and sheer humidity—Ana could recall the sensory overload as if it was yesterday. It had been the first time her hair had felt like a heavy, thick burden, and she'd vowed there and then to chop it off at the first opportunity.

That had been the start of her metamorphosis from being a tomboy who'd hidden behind her brothers all her life into her own woman. *Seeking Caio's attention had also been a motivator.* Her conscience pricked. Yes. She had wanted to lure his eye, not liking how invisible she felt when she stood beside him in public...

But she didn't want to think about that now.

One evening Caio had returned to the hotel suite from a business meeting to find Ana pacing up and down, so full of rage and a sense of helplessness that she wasn't even aware she'd been crying.

'What is it? What's happened?' he'd asked.

She'd been so angry she hardly been able to speak. He'd made her sit down, given her a glass of water, and then she'd explained that her father had reneged on his agreement to send her younger brother to art school in Holland.

It shouldn't have surprised her that her father was capable of that, but it was the reason she'd agreed to marry Caio Salazar. Caio had asked her what she wanted in return for marrying him, and he'd promised to extract an agreement from her father that he would not stand in the way of Francisco's dream to attend art college.

Caio had gone very still and left the room for a long moment. When he'd come back his tie had been off, and his jacket gone, shirt open. He'd poured himself a whiskey and said, 'Call your brother tomorrow and let him know he's still going to Holland. Nothing will stand in his way again.'

That had been the first time Ana had seen a different side to Caio and felt some sort of kinship. She'd had a strong sense that he was almost as angry as she that her father had reneged on the agreement. It had made her wonder about Caio's relationship with his own family…only his mother had come to their wedding…

After that night, Ana had become more and more aware that the image of man she'd thought Caio was—a jaded playboy pretending to reform for the sake of his ambitions— was not truly reflective of the man she was coming to know.

For instance, he'd never seemed to mind that his life was suddenly devoid of loud thumping nightclubs and glamorous premieres. The events they'd attended had been on the more sedate and serious side.

He'd proved himself to be nothing like the

men she knew—her father and older brothers. And, contrary to his infamous persona as a louche playboy, he'd either been the most discreet man on the planet or he'd embraced a year of domesticity and celibacy, showing a far more introverted side than the world at large would have expected of him.

She knew better than anyone how the press could magnify a situation and turn it into something lurid. Like when her mother had walked out on her family.

She'd left because she was bored. She'd felt she'd done her duty, providing an heir and some spares. And so she'd left. It had been devastating to Ana, to realise how little her mother loved her, and the rest of her siblings. Her father hadn't been under any illusions—it had been an arranged marriage, after all. But his pride had been wounded.

The press had had a field-day, painting a melodramatic picture of a woman seeking love and solace with a younger and even richer man. Ana knew that it hadn't been a lack of love driving her mother—it had been dissatisfaction and boredom—but they'd spun it into something else entirely, the truth being too prosaic and cynical.

Ana shook her head, as if that could clear the toxic memories. She refocused on the memory of Caio coolly taking her father to task for not following through on his agreement.

Now she felt even more churlish for not joining Caio for lunch. She should go back.

She stood up, took a few steps, and stopped. Maybe she was better just to avoid him... After all, when this was over and they returned to Rio she wouldn't see him again. So why bother to make any effort now?

You just don't want him to find out how much you want him, whispered a mocking little voice.

Ana was making a face at herself when she heard a sound and looked up to see a vision of masculine perfection, largely naked but for a short pair of snug swim-trunks, striding out from the trees onto the beach, a towel slung over his shoulder, shades covering his eyes.

He might as well have been naked for all the trunks barely covered. They only drew attention to the perfect curvature of Caio's muscular buttocks.

The breath stopped in Ana's throat. She must have made some sort of gurgling sound, because Caio glanced at her but didn't seem surprised she was there. He said, off-handedly, 'I figured it's best to swim before eating. Join me if you like.'

Ana was no more capable of joining Caio

than she was of moving. She managed to garble something about seeing to lunch and stumbled backwards, unable to take her eyes off the acres of gleaming olive skin moving smoothly over taut muscles.

Oblivious to the nuclear explosion happening inside Ana, Caio threw the towel and sunglasses down on the sand and launched himself into the water, arms scissoring powerfully through the waves.

The cooler confines of the open-plan kitchen were no comfort to Ana's hot and prickling skin, which had nothing to do with the sun and everything to do with Caio's little exhibition back there.

She paced the space; the tiles were cool underfoot but provided no relief. Anger rose. Did he have no idea how that might affect her? Seeing all that naked flesh on display? Seeing the prominent bulge at the front of his shorts that left little to the imagination?

Her face flamed. Not that she needed her imagination for that. She'd seen him in the flesh.

This really was peak humiliation. Proof that she made so little impact on him that walking around in front of her half-naked was the equivalent of being in a locker room full of guys at his gym. Not that he went to a gym, because he had his own gym, but—

Ana scowled and shook her head. *Not the point here!*

The point was that she affected him so minutely that she could have been sunbathing naked on the beach for all he'd have noticed her as being a breathing, sexual woman. A woman who had hidden her responses to him so well that he now saw her as little more than furniture.

And who was to blame for that? Not Caio. Much as it pained her to admit it. He didn't fancy her. Simple as that. And brutal as that.

She stopped pacing. She felt constricted in her clothes now. The silk shirt was clinging to her skin and the trousers digging in at her waist.

On an impulse she went up to the bedroom suite and looked at the clothes.

She noticed for the first time that there were evening dresses in the guests' section. A glimmering opulent royal blue caught her eye. She reached in to pull the dress out. It was silk, and slippery through her fingers. It was stunningly simple but devastatingly sexy. A halter-neck design, with a deep vee in the front, almost down to the navel.

Ana's skin grew hot at the thought of wearing this in front of Caio, of baring so much skin.

She'd been growing more adventurous with her dresses of late, in a shameful and fruitless attempt on her part to see if she had any effect on him at all. She'd worn a red dress to a recent event. Very simple, with spaghetti straps, a chiffon overlay had hugged her torso tight and criss-crossed over her chest with the beaded material exposed over one breast as a contrast, drawing the eye. It had had a thigh-high slit.

She'd drawn lots of eyes that night, but every time she'd sneaked a glance at Caio his jaw had been like granite and his face expressionless. His lack of reaction had made her feel reckless. Volatile. But when they'd returned to the apartment that night he'd said something about working and disappeared into his study to make calls—presumably to the other side of the world, where they were just waking up.

Her volatility had drained away. How could she have forgotten that her primary role in his life was to enhance his career?

Not that she could blame him—it wasn't as if she'd ever been under any illusions in that regard. In their world, a strategic marriage was part of the natural order.

But that reckless feeling was back now, rising inside her. Dangerous. Maybe it was the knowledge that they were divorced. And on a desert island. In the middle of the sea. Nowhere to go and nothing to lose.

Except your dignity.

Ana ignored the voice, even though she knew in her heart of hearts that, as volatile as she felt, she didn't really have the nerve to put herself out there. To really test the waters. As much as she'd love to unsettle him as he unsettled her. As much as she wanted him to look at her with the same hunger she felt.

But then he hadn't even looked at her differently after her transformation at the hands of London's finest stylists and beauty technicians.

As if she needed *that* humiliating reminder…

CHAPTER SIX

AFTER BANGKOK THEY'D gone to London. The first event they'd attended there had been in the glittering ballroom of one of London's most iconic and luxurious hotels. By then Ana had been feeling more comfortable with Caio in social surroundings, while also becoming more and more aware that she was drawing looks not because she was stylish, but because she didn't fit in with all the other sleek and fashionable women.

When she'd overheard a woman say, not so discreetly, 'That's his wife? I thought Brazilian women were meant to be sexy and beautiful? She looks like she's just been released from a convent...' Ana had made an appointment the following day for a makeover in the hotel salon, knowing full well that her motivation stemmed more from a desire to please Caio than any bitchy gossips.

After a day of being primped, plucked and

styled to within an inch of her life, Ana had waited nervously for Caio that evening to meet her in the reception room of the suite before going to a charity gala dinner. She'd been wearing a strapless black cocktail dress so form-fitting that she'd constantly felt like tugging it up over her chest, or down over her knee. Heels so high they'd made her eyes water.

But that dress hadn't been the thing making her feel naked. It had been her hair. Or the lack of it. It was the first time she'd had it cut substantially in her life. Because from the day her mother had left she'd used it as a shield to hide behind. To hide her grief. Her anger. Her burgeoning sexuality. Her vulnerabilities.

But now it was gone. Now it feathered lightly over her shoulders where only hours before it had fallen down to the middle of her back. And at any minute Caio was going to appear...

And then he had. Looking at his cufflinks. Not at Ana, where she'd stood trembling.

Finally, he'd looked up, saying, 'Ready?'

His dark eyes had narrowed on her and Ana's pulse-rate had sky-rocketed.

After a long moment he'd said, 'You look different.'

Ana had thought of how she'd reacted when

she'd seen herself in the mirror a short time before. She hadn't looked like herself at all. Or she had. But a much sleeker version. Her eyes had looked huge. Her lips red.

The hair stylist had said, mock severely, 'It's criminal you've hidden this face for so long. You are stunning.'

Ana had smiled weakly, feeling exposed, but also a fluttering sense of hope that maybe now Caio would look at her with interest. Sexual interest.

Except he hadn't looked at her with sexual interest. He'd looked at her with an expression she couldn't read. He'd looked tense. A muscle had pulsed in his jaw.

Ana had swallowed her disappointment and said, 'I got my hair cut…consulted with a stylist about some new clothes.'

Sounding almost accusing, Caio had said, 'You're wearing make-up.'

Ana had said defensively, 'Not a lot, actually.'

The make-up artist had said to her, 'You really don't need much at all…just enough to emphasise those big eyes and your mouth. You know, women spend a fortune to get lips like yours…'

Feeling hurt at the thought that Caio had somehow preferred her when she'd been hiding behind her hair and wearing unflattering clothes, Ana had said testily, 'If you don't think I look okay—'

But he'd cut her off, saying stiffly, 'You look…fine. We need to leave or we'll be late.'

And that had been that.

Caio's less than thrilled reaction to her transformation.

But over the months, in spite of Caio's reaction, Ana had grown in confidence and had found that she preferred a kind of timeless elegant style. The stylist she'd worked with in London had become a friend, and Ana had used her expertise to help her find outfits for various events, working with her remotely.

But now…

Ana let the liquid silk of the beautiful blue dress slip out of her hand. It was good that she'd remembered Caio's reaction to her transformation. No matter how reckless she might feel, it didn't change the fact that he wasn't interested.

She went to her own clothes and pulled out a pair of worn cut-off shorts and a T-shirt. It wasn't as if he'd even notice if she put on that dress anyway, so why bother?

She hadn't worn clothes like this for a long time now. Being married to Caio had morphed her into someone different. *Or someone more herself?* It was a persona she hadn't been comfortable with at first, but now it felt more familiar to her than her old tomboy self ever had.

Leaving her feet bare, Ana went down to the kitchen, relieved to see that it was empty. Caio must still be at the beach. She saw that he'd taken some things out of the fridge—the makings of a salad. She took it upon herself to put the ingredients together, mixing up a light lemony vinaigrette and chopping up tomato, avocado, cucumber, adding some nuts and grapes.

She warmed some crusty bread in the oven, and nearly jumped out of her skin when a deep voice said from behind her, 'Changed your mind, then?'

Ana whirled around to see Caio standing a few feet away, wearing faded jeans and a T-shirt. Like her. His hair was damp. He must have come back and taken a shower. How long had he been there? Why hadn't she heard him?

She looked down. Bare feet like her. Except his were about seven sizes bigger than hers. He was big all over.

A wave of heat exploded in her belly. Her brain felt fuzzy. 'Changed my mind...?'

He gestured to the kitchen island. 'Lunch.'

Ana looked at the salad blankly for a moment before her brain switched back into gear. She affected a little shrug, as if she hadn't just had a brain meltdown just because Caio was in the room. It was as if a layer of protection had been ripped off her skin here on this island.

'I figured I might as well start getting it together. Unless you had something else in mind?'

He shook his head, looking at the salad. 'This is exactly what I envisaged, but I wouldn't have put it together as well as this. You have a real talent. I never did ask where you learned to cook...'

Ana had not been expecting that. Over the year, when they'd been in Rio de Janeiro, and if there hadn't been a function to go to, Ana had got used to letting the chef go and cooking herself. At first Caio hadn't joined her, but as time had passed it had become habitual for them to share meals.

Caio settled on a high stool on the other side of the island and picked up the lone grape left in a bowl, 'You know, I only recently realised that it was you cooking those meals and not the chef. I thought he was leaving food for you to heat up.'

Ana cut up rough hunks of bread, hating it that she still felt self-conscious under Caio's inquisitive gaze. 'I learnt how to cook because I knew it would annoy my father. He was horrified at the thought of me doing anything remotely domestic or manual, and as my life pretty much revolved around irritating him as much as I could...' She trailed off, realising that she must sound like a petulant teenager.

She busied herself carrying the salad in a bowl over to the kitchen's dining table.

Caio followed with the bread and asked, 'Would you like some wine?'

That dangerous flash of recklessness gripped her again. 'Sure.'

She grabbed some sparkling water and glasses, watching as Caio took a bottle of chilled white wine out of the fridge and brought it over. He pulled out the cork with an ease and dexterity that really shouldn't be sexy, but even that caused a spiking of need deep inside Ana.

When it was poured, she took a gulp of wine in a bid to try and cool her wayward hormones. It had to be just a heightened reaction to the adrenalin of the morning—that was all.

The dry, crisp taste of the wine slid down her throat and went straight to her head. Probably not the best idea around Caio, who was taking a sip of his own wine, the glass looking very fragile in his big hand.

She mixed up the salad with two spoons and said, 'Help yourself.'

Caio heaped salad onto his plate and drizzled some olive oil over his bread. He said idly, 'You really hate your father, don't you?'

Ana almost choked on her mouthful of food and had to swallow carefully. 'It's that obvious?' she joked.

Caio shrugged. 'I saw it the day we met, and since then you've made little or no effort to see him.'

Ana took another sip of wine, put her glass down. 'I can't say I feel any great affection for him, no. Me and my younger brother were superfluous to his requirements. My only value to him was as a marriageable asset. I have enough older brothers to ensure the family legacy is taken care of.'

'You and your younger brother are obviously close.'

She nodded, immediately feeling protective. 'Very. There's only a year between us. I was six and he was five when our mother left.'

This was said with as little emotion as possible. Ana hated it that even now the memory of watching her mother pack and leave without a backward glance was still so vivid. She felt raw.

'What about you?' she asked. 'Only your

mother came to the wedding—you're not close to the rest of your family?'

Caio's face tightened for a moment and then he said, 'Like you, I was considered superfluous to requirements. My father and mother... it was an arranged marriage.'

Aren't they all? Ana wanted to say, but didn't.

Caio didn't seem inclined to elaborate on his parents' marriage beyond that.

'How old were you when you left home?' she asked.

He looked at her. 'Eighteen.'

'That's when you dropped your father's name?'

He nodded. And then he said, 'Surely you could have left too?'

Ana shook her head. 'I wouldn't have left Francisco on his own.'

'Does he know you agreed to our marriage to secure his freedom?'

Ana felt like squirming. How had they strayed into this territory when for the last year they'd managed to keep their conversations light and superficial? But here, on this island, it was as if all normal operations had been left back in Rio.

Ana huffed out a breath. 'He knows. And he only agreed to go to Europe once he knew the marriage was strictly business and only for a year.' She looked at Caio, feeling defensive. 'He would have done the same for me.'

Caio's lips twitched at the corners. 'I don't doubt it.'

Ana put a forkful of salad in her mouth in case she said anything else or invited the conversation into more personal territory. She'd known that Caio had a very tenuous connection with his family, and even without him elaborating on details, it sounded like it had been a very similar situation. People still whispered and gossiped about her mother's abandonment of her family, and the subsequent bitter divorce, even though it had happened years ago. Ana had never heard any gossip about his family. Presumably they'd been more careful because they were involved in politics.

But then his mother hadn't abandoned her family like Ana's had. Was it better for a mother to be a martyr to an arranged marriage or selfish enough to leave for her own happiness? She and Caio were products of each scenario, and she realised now that it might not have necessarily been better if her mother had stayed. She recalled meeting Caio's mother—she'd seemed very fragile, brittle. Like a shadow of a former self.

Caio put down his fork and it made a slight metallic sound against the plate, breaking Ana out of her reverie. She wasn't remotely prepared when he asked, 'Was it really so bad that you had to leave Rio today?'

CHAPTER SEVEN

ANA NEARLY CHOKED on her food. She swallowed carefully as she let his question sink in. Why did she feel so guilty and defensive?

Caio was looking at her. Waiting. Her impression of him being hurt because she was so eager to leave returned. But that couldn't be right.

She wiped her mouth with a napkin. 'No, not at all. Like I said... I didn't know what to expect at first, but as the year went on we...' She trailed off. *Became unlikely friends.*

Caio's face was expressionless. She was beginning to understand that this didn't necessarily mean he didn't feel anything. A little muscle pulsed by his jaw.

She said with a rush, 'I thought that you wanted to get your life back as soon as possible.'

'Did I make you feel unwelcome?'

Ana wanted to squirm. The problem had

been *her*, not him. 'No. It wasn't that. At all. I wasn't expecting that the marriage would turn out the way it did.' She looked at him 'We got on,' she said, surprising herself.

'I thought so. We worked a room well together.'

A flush of warmth that had nothing to do with desire bloomed in Ana's chest. At first she'd been so awkward on Caio's arm. Felt out of place. Which was ironic given that they'd been in the milieu she'd been born to command as her own. But she'd spent so much time rebelling against the etiquette and social lessons her peers had lapped up, she'd felt about as prepared as an alien visiting earth for the first time.

But gradually, with a discreet guidance from Caio that Ana could appreciate now, she'd grown more adept. She thought of how with the subtlest of touches and glances, silent commands or needs had been communicated between them, fostering a sense of unity that she hadn't fully appreciated until this moment.

'We did work a room well together,' she had to admit grudgingly. She gave a small shudder, 'Remember those couples who'd obviously just had a blazing row and were forced to smile and act as if everything was okay?'

'When it patently wasn't? No, thanks.'

'You never wanted to get married for real, then?' She'd always just assumed that once he had all his ambitions met he would settle down.

'After what I've seen? No way. Happy marriages don't exist. It's fantasy.'

Ana agreed with Caio intellectually, but deep in her gut told another story. She wanted to ask him what he had seen, but reticence held her back.

He continued before she could work up the nerve to speak, saying, 'That's why a marriage of convenience worked so well for us.'

'I can remember the tension between my parents after massive arguments,' Ana observed. 'Moments before a dinner party. And theirs was an arranged marriage.'

Caio took a sip of wine. 'Ah, but children complicate things.'

She hid a dart of hurt to think of how she and her siblings obviously hadn't complicated things enough to make her mother stay.

Ana pulled a knee up and rested her foot on the chair, wrapping her arms around her leg. She felt emboldened enough by Caio's candour to ask, 'You never wanted children?'

For a split-second Ana could have sworn she saw something like yearning cross Caio's face, as if she'd caught him off guard. But then it was gone.

'No. I didn't see enough of good, positive parenting to be able to pass it on. It wouldn't be fair.'

Not sure where her doggedness was coming from, Ana said, 'But what's the point, then, of building up a business in your own name, if you can't leave it to anyone?'

Caio's focus narrowed on her face. She grew warm.

He said, almost chidingly, 'Having children is no guarantee that they'll want to follow in your footsteps. Not one of my brothers is really interested in the family business but they had no choice. It was accept it or lose your inheritance.'

Ana murmured, 'And you took the latter option?'

Caio said, 'I was lucky to be able to. The pressure wasn't on me.'

Ana had a sense, though, that even if the pressure had been on him he would have gone his own way. Nothing would have stopped him. He was too strong to be bent to anyone's will.

'Do *you* want children?' Caio asked.

Ana's insides clenched. Her dream was too secret and fragile to articulate. Instead, she prevaricated. 'Like you, I didn't exactly grow up with good role models.' She looked around the kitchen area and said, 'But I think this place, this island, is an example that it can exist for some people.'

Caio shrugged and took another sip of wine. 'Who knows what Luca Fonseca's marriage is like…? I'd bet it's not as idyllic as you think.'

His persistent cynicism rubbed along Ana's nerve-endings. 'This place feels *real*. It's not for show. It's for them.'

Caio's mouth quirked. 'Don't tell me you're a closet romantic?'

CHAPTER EIGHT

ANA'S HEART STUTTERED. She was exposing herself.

She sprang up from the chair as if stung and started clearing the plates. 'Don't be ridiculous. I know better than anyone that fairy tales don't exist. That's why I agreed to marry you—to extract as much leverage as I could.'

She took the plates over to the island and put them down with a clatter. She felt brittle all of a sudden.

'So if your aim was to extract as much leverage as possible, why didn't you fleece me for all that you could get?'

Ana turned around and put her hands behind her, wrapping her fingers around the edge of the marble countertop. Caio had angled his chair to face her, his big body sprawled with elegant insouciance, the wine glass between his fingers. He was enjoying this. Damn him.

'Because I'm not mercenary. If I've learned

anything about our lives, our world, it's that money doesn't buy happiness. Fulfilling personal dreams does. Finding your freedom does.'

'So what *are* your personal dreams? You've facilitated your brother's, but what about yours?'

Ana's face grew hot again. She wanted to escape this conversation that seemed determined to stray into territory more personal than she'd shared with Caio in a whole year. It was as if the divorce and being sequestered on this island had ripped away any need to tread carefully around each other. It was as exhilarating as it was terrifying.

She lifted her chin and pushed down the sense of exposure. 'I want to get a degree.'

Caio looked at Ana. He'd never seen her look so fierce. Well, he had—the night she'd agreed to marry him if it meant she could guarantee her brother the future he wanted.

Her fierceness made his blood simmer, while also catching at his chest. She reminded him of a cornered kitten, all at once defensive and proud. She looked a little wild. Undone. Reminding him of the girl he'd first met. Prickly. Combative. Distrustful. He was fascinated by her reaction.

'So what do you want to do a degree in?' he asked.

She shrugged, her face pink now. 'I've always wanted to do an English degree. In England.' She blurted the last bit out, then said in a rush, 'But I'm not remotely cut out for university. No woman in my family has ever gone to university.'

Caio felt a surge of anger on her behalf. 'Why would you think you're not suited to it?'

'Because I was never academic. I barely scraped through my exams each year. As my father liked to tell me, paying for my education was a waste of time and money.'

Caio shook his head. 'I bet he didn't say that to your brothers.'

Ana smiled, but it was tight. 'Of course not. They weren't the brightest either, but he made sure they got degrees from the best North American universities.'

Caio sat forward. 'Ana, I can guarantee you that you're brighter than all your brothers put together. I've met them. I know what I'm talking about.'

A surprised giggle escaped Ana's mouth and she put her hand over it. The movement lifted her T-shirt, revealing a sliver of flat belly above her shorts. Caio's mouth dried. He dragged his gaze up again, over the swells of her plump breasts under the thin material. He could see the outline of her very plain bra. She shouldn't be arousing this raging fire inside him, but she was.

He met her gaze. It was serious now. She took her hand down and Caio looked at her mouth. Provocative. Lush. Why on earth hadn't he tasted her when he'd had a chance? He couldn't fathom it now.

'Anyway,' she said, 'there's not a hope that I'd get accepted on the basis of my exam results. It's a pipe dream.'

Caio made a noise. 'Don't be so defeatist. You could apply as a mature student, and lots of universities accept students based on their current aptitude and desire to do a course, more than past results.'

'I'd only accept a course on that basis, I wouldn't want to buy my place just because I can.'

Caio felt a spike of admiration at Ana's evident pride and desire to prove herself. He'd met very few people like her in his world. Most of them were only too eager to catch a free ride or take advantage of their wealth and influence. But not Ana.

Her integrity mocked his habitual cynicism. It made him feel weary. It made him conscious of this place-Ana was right—this island and villa oozed a kind of peace and contentment he'd never felt in a home before. It caught at him, made him wonder about another type of existence where you were born into a world where legacy, ambition, greed and cynicism weren't the natural order. Where something else was. *Family.* Unconditional love. Acceptance.

Caio mentally shook his head to dislodge those rogue ideas. He'd been born into an extremely privileged world and, while he'd made his own way in the end, he'd be delusional not to acknowledge that he'd still achieved much of his success off the back of who he was. He didn't need warm and fluffy family values. He needed his wits and his business acumen.

Ana turned away from him and his gaze caught on her shapely bare legs. Toned and slim. The bottom of her shorts was just short enough to give a hint of her buttocks. High and curved.

A solid knot of need tightened in his gut. It was bizarre, this attraction. It had been there from the moment he'd seen her, if he was honest, and she wasn't remotely his type. He'd always gone for women who were taller. Women whose expressions were as carefully schooled as his. Women who were experienced…who knew the game.

Ana was the very antithesis of all that.

Caio broke out of his reverie when he saw Ana pick up the plates again. He put down his glass and stood up to help her, reaching for them and saying, 'Here, let me do that.'

Ana turned around and wasn't expecting Caio to be right behind her, hands outstretched. It all happened so fast it was a blur. But, mortifyingly, she knew even in that moment that it was his proximity that caused it. The plates toppled out of her suddenly unsteady hands and fell to the floor, smashing to pieces.

She immediately bent down and put out a hand to pick up part of a plate. She felt a sting in her finger.

'Leave it—you've cut yourself.' Caio's voice was sharp.

Before she knew which way was up, Caio had his hands under her arms and was pulling her up, then lifting her into his arms to step over the smashed debris to the sink.

'Your feet are bare too,' she protested weakly, rendered insensible by the fact that she was pressed close to his chest and it felt so broad and hard. His arms were like steel bands around her.

'I'm fine.'

He put her down by the sink and Ana had

to lock her knees to stop herself crumpling like a doll. Blood was oozing from the top of her finger. Caio had her hand in his and was putting it under running water.

'I need to make sure there's no splinter.'

He was gentle, but thorough. Ana could hardly breathe, but she managed to say, 'Since when did you know so much about first aid?'

His face tightened. 'Let's just say it was a skill I had to learn.'

Suddenly Ana went still, as something occurred to her. Had there been violence in his family?

Caio shut off the water and said briskly, 'Keep your hand raised while I look for a plaster. It's not a deep cut.'

He turned away to open a cupboard and pulled out a box with the universal symbol for first aid on the side. It was well-stocked, and full of things Ana wouldn't have known how to use, but Caio found the plasters and caught her hand again.

But then he stopped.

Ana looked down to see a fresh bead of blood on her finger. Caio said in a rough-sounding voice, 'I need to clean it first.'

But he wasn't moving. He was just looking at her. Ana couldn't look away. His eyes held her captive. They were molten again, like when she'd seen him naked.

She hadn't imagined it.

He moved then, tugging her back towards the tap, but she said, 'Wait, I can do it.' Acting on instinct, she lifted her finger and put the tip into her mouth, sucking it clean.

The air contracted around them. Caio's eyes weren't molten any more. They were burning. She took her finger out of her mouth and held it up, pink and moist. No blood.

They were so close that if Ana moved an inch forward the tips of her breasts would come into contact with Caio's chest. Heat suffused her whole body and made her feel both energised and incredibly languorous. Something had just shifted between them, and it was monumental. She was afraid to say a word in case she broke the spell. It thrummed in her blood like a drumbeat.

He wanted her. *He wanted her.*

But even as that thought registered, and a surge of excitement and exhilaration made her limbs tremble, Caio broke eye contact and took a step back. He caught Ana's hand again and deftly wrapped a plaster around her finger before she could take another breath. She felt dizzy at the speed with which he'd gone from hot to cold. It almost made her think she'd imagined it—*but she hadn't*. She'd seen it, *felt it*. Could still feel it in her blood.

Caio was avoiding her eye now. He said briskly, 'I'll clean this mess up. You should put some shoes on until I get all the shards.'

Ana felt too unsettled to argue. She left the kitchen and went up to her bedroom, pacing up and down, jittery. She *had* seen it…felt it. There had been something between them. It was as if a veil had been pulled back for a moment and the depth of Caio's desire had been revealed and it was actually…overwhelming.

And yet he'd shut it down. Clearly giving her the option of pretending she hadn't noticed.

Her mind raced—how long had he felt like this?

Ana took a deep breath. If she wasn't imagining this, and if Caio did want her, then this was huge. She was pretty certain she hadn't been as adept as he when it came to hiding her desire. How could she have been? Compared with him she was…*a virgin*.

Ana sat down heavily on the bed. Maybe the thought of initiating a novice just didn't appeal. Not to a man as experienced as him. He would want a lover who knew exactly how to give him what he desired in the shortest amount of time possible. After all, he had told her in no uncertain terms that he didn't sleep with virgins, and clearly that had overridden any desire he felt.

Ana thought of a lurid piece of gossip she'd read when he'd first appeared at their house to do business with her father. Two women—famous supermodels—had sold their story of a steamy night spent with Caio Salazar, mentioning breathlessly how insatiable he'd been and how they'd never experienced such pleasure…

How could she compete with two supermodels and a threesome? But then they weren't here…and she was. And, unless she was very mistaken, Caio had been as celibate as she for this last year.

Which meant that surely his level of control wasn't all that strong? Even if she was a virgin?

That heady recklessness gripped her and this time she didn't try and stop it. Caio wanted her. She was sure of it. They were alone on this island for twenty-four hours. Less, actually. They'd already been here for a few hours. No distractions. No interruptions. Nothing to lose.

Things were very clear to her now. Time was running out and she did not want to be a virgin when she left this island to embark on her new life. And she wanted Caio Salazar, her ex-husband, to be her first lover.

Wanting him and trying to hide it had become a daily battle. But she didn't have to battle it any more. Not if she seduced him.

The thought was so audacious that a semi-hysterical giggle rose up Ana's throat. She put a hand over her mouth to try and contain it.

Serious again, she took her hand down. Caio would not make it easy for her. For whatever reason, he'd kept to his vow for the year, and he hadn't touched her beyond what had been required in public. She would have to work to seduce him. And maybe it would be humiliating if he had stronger control than she gave him credit for.

But…was her dignity really so important? She'd never have to see him again after this night.

She needed to challenge him. To know for sure.

Before she lost her nerve, Ana got up and went into the dressing room. She wasn't even sure what she was looking for, but when she saw it she knew that it was perfect.

CHAPTER NINE

CAIO FELT UNEASY. There was a prickling awareness under his skin. *Ana knew.* She'd seen his hunger because, standing that close to her, he hadn't been able to hide it. The control he'd clung to for months now was snapping and fraying.

All he could see in his mind's eye were those huge brown eyes as she'd sucked the tip of her finger into her mouth. Like a practised seductress. Which he knew she wasn't because, unless she'd employed the stealth of a secret service agent, she was still the virgin she'd been on her wedding night. It had taken him every ounce of effort not to replace her finger with his mouth and tongue, delving deep into the sweetness he'd been dreaming about.

Except the word 'dreaming' was too benign. They were hot, sweaty and X-rated sleeping hallucinations. And, even worse, they'd become fantasies of being the first man to possess her fully. To see her face flush and her eyes grow wide when her first orgasm hit.

Stupid, Caio castigated himself now, in a bid to try and cool his body down. She might be a virgin, but a woman of her age would have fooled around at least, and would have been brought to orgasm many times. Even by her own hand.

Heat fused his brain at the thought of Ana pleasuring herself. *Deus!*

He ran a hand through his hair. He'd cleared up the detritus of the broken plates. He felt edgy. Restless. *Frustrated.* They were mere hours into their enforced confinement on this island and he was losing it already.

He went out through the French doors that led out to the sloping manicured lawn. The pool glinted invitingly.

Caio thought about diving under the water again—anything to try and cool the heat in his blood. But he'd just eaten. *Not a good idea.*

He heard a sound from behind him, and with a feeling of intense trepidation turned around.

When Caio took in the view before him the

first thought in his head was that he would never, as long as he lived, erase this image from his brain.

Ana's heart was pounding. So much for aiming for nonchalance. Suddenly she felt very exposed.

Not hard, considering that she was wearing precisely three small triangles of white material that were held together at the front, at her midriff, by a silver and diamond-encrusted circlet, and at her neck by a halter-neck fastening. Dangling from the silver circlet at her midriff, a delicate diamond chain circled her waist. Wedge sandals elevated her a few precious inches.

Not even the sunglasses she wore could protect her from the shock emanating from Caio's rigid body as he turned to look at her. Shock… and also scorching heat. Ana could feel it lick over her skin in little tongues of sensation.

She hadn't imagined it.

Exhilaration coursed through her blood.

She'd tied a short diaphanous wrap around her hips in a bid to preserve some modesty, but she knew well that it only highlighted the scantiness of her outfit.

She'd plucked a random book off the shelf

in the den and held it up now as evidence. 'I thought I'd lie by the pool for a bit.'

'It's after midday…the sun is high.'

There was a rough quality to Caio's voice that made her skin raise up into goosebumps.

'I've put on sunscreen. I'm not careless. And I'm planning on lying in the shade.'

She walked towards Caio, her legs feeling embarrassingly shaky. He watched her with such a brooding expression on his face that she was glad she was wearing sunglasses.

She skirted around him. 'I'll just dump my things and come back for a drink.'

'What would you like? I'll bring it out.'

Ana desperately wanted to emulate Caio's usual lovers and say something sophisticated like, *A glass of champagne, darling* or, *A cocktail, of course. I'll let you decide.* But she was no hardened drinker at the best of times, and in this current mood and climate, alcohol would not be her friend.

'A sparkling water is fine.'

She walked down to the pool, aware of Caio's gaze burning into her very bare back. From behind, she knew that it would look as if she wasn't wearing anything but briefs and that piece of wispy material. And the diamond chain.

By the time she got to the pool she all but

fell onto a lounger. She could barely keep it together under Caio's gaze—what would it be like if he actually touched her? Kissed her?

He appeared now, striding across the lawn towards her with a glass of water, looking like a very stern waiter. A very sexy stern waiter.

She hurriedly arranged herself in as languid a fashion as possible, as if this was entirely habitual for her and not a desperate attempt to seduce her ex-husband.

She could sense him standing beside her and after a moment she stirred, as if she'd had her eyes closed, and pushed her sunglasses onto her head. 'Sorry, I didn't see you there.'

She reached out for the glass, but Caio held it aloft. His jaw was tight. Ana's hand dropped.

'What are you up to, Ana?'

She was determined not to let the fact that she was so obviously acting out of character put her off. She widened her eyes the way she'd seen hundreds of women do when talking to Caio. Her presence had never made any difference.

'I don't know what you're talking about.'

He sat down abruptly on the lounger beside hers. She noticed that he kept his gaze up. He put the glass down on the table between them.

He waved a hand towards her. 'What's…this?'

A spark of fire lit up Ana's insides when she thought of her reaction to him on the beach earlier. 'Swimwear, Caio. I'm sure you've seen a vast array on plenty of women in your lifetime. It's no more or less revealing that what you yourself were wearing earlier, when you took your swim.'

A strangled sound came from Caio's throat. Then, 'I've seen you wearing swimwear before, and you usually prefer one-pieces.'

Do I, now? thought Ana, as that rebellious spirit filled her. She sensed a desperation in Caio.

She sat up on the lounger and put her hands behind her, so that her chest thrust forward a little. 'Technically, this is a one-piece…with bits cut out.'

The effort it was taking for Caio not to let his gaze drop to take in the plump swells of Ana's high, firm breasts, threatening to burst free from the minuscule pieces of material covering them, was making sweat break out on his brow.

He had been around women a long time. With older brothers who'd been a target for status-climbing socialites, he'd seen a lot, and had been initiated himself at a young age. For years now women had ceased to do much more than spark a modicum of interest in him.

That had been another factor in why a marriage of convenience to Ana Diaz had appealed. The thought of not having to play that tiresome game for a while. But right now he realised he'd made a huge error of judgement—because, contrary to his assumption that marriage to her would be a break, his awareness of her had been a constant, growing thing, and right now it was all he could see and feel.

He was consumed.

He'd been an arrogant fool and now he was paying for it.

She asked pertly, 'How is this different to what you were wearing earlier when you went for a swim?'

Heat was melting Caio's brain. He shook his head. 'It's different.'

She snorted. 'Typical double standards.'

Caio opened his mouth, but he realised that he didn't want to speak. He wanted to stop the words coming out of Ana's mouth by crushing it under his, and then he wanted to pull aside those excuses for pieces of material and feast on her breasts until she was writhing against him with need, and then he wanted to explore between her legs to see how responsive she was—

Suficiente!

Caio stood up abruptly. He felt dizzy with the strength of need coursing through his blood. 'Of course you can wear what you want.'

He turned and took a couple of steps, but then Ana said from behind him, 'Wait.'

He didn't turn around.

'What I wear shouldn't bother you... Unless it bothers you because...' There was silence, and then Ana said in a rush, 'Because maybe you want me.'

CHAPTER TEN

ANA'S HEART WAS pounding so hard she was sure Caio must be able to hear it. He still had his back to her. She thought he might just ignore her, walk away. The ultimate humiliation. But then he turned around slowly.

Every line of his body was tense. She'd never seen his face so stark. His eyes were dark and unreadable from here.

'Ana…'

She held her breath.

'This isn't about me wanting you. You are a beautiful woman. Very desirable. I'm not made of stone. Of course I'm…aware of you…'

All she heard for a long, dizzying second was *very desirable*. He thought she was desirable. Beautiful. Ana couldn't breathe.

'…not going to happen.'

Ana blinked. She'd missed whatever Caio

had been saying due to the rush of blood to her head. 'What's not going to happen?'

He gestured with a hand between them. 'This. Us.'

'Why not?'

Caio's jaw clenched. 'Because it's not a good idea. We were married. We had a relationship.'

Ana stood up. 'You do realise how crazy that sounds? If anything, it's stranger that we didn't consummate the marriage.'

Caio's gaze narrowed on her face. 'You made it pretty clear on our wedding night that you weren't interested in consummating the marriage.'

Ana flushed when she recalled her feeling of panic that Caio would realise how much she wanted him. 'That's not fair. I told you I had no idea what kind of person you were. What you'd expect.'

A look of disgust flashed across his face. 'I've never forced a woman to do anything against her will, and I wasn't about to start when we got married.'

Ana bit her lip. This wasn't going at all the way she'd envisaged. 'No, I know. And I never thought you were capable of...*that*.'

'What was it, then?'

Ana looked at Caio. She was practically

naked. She had nowhere to hide. She took a breath. 'I was afraid you'd realise how much I... I fancied you. That it would be...humiliating.'

Caio shook his head. 'I wouldn't have humiliated you.'

A memory popped into Ana's head. 'I was certain you didn't want me. That you were immune to me. At that cancer charity benefit last month you were so tense. You could barely touch me. I thought it was because you couldn't wait to see the back of me.'

That had been a low moment for Ana—the realisation that Caio must be counting down the days to when he was free again. Free of this arrangement with his convenient wife.

But he shook his head, his mouth tight. 'Definitely not immune.'

Ana's pulse tripped. She lifted her chin. 'So why not...now?' *Was he going to make her beg?* 'We're two consenting adults. No one needs to know. I know I'm not your usual type, if that's what you're—'

Caio put up a hand. 'I have a type?'

Ana lifted a shoulder. 'Tall, skinny... Beautiful.'

'There's no comparison,' Caio said abruptly.

This really wasn't going well. Ana wished she had a long voluminous cardigan to wrap around her body. 'I know. You don't need to remind me of that.'

Caio took a step towards her. She looked up.

'No, I didn't mean it like that.' He stopped and ran a hand through his hair. 'I meant that you shouldn't compare yourself with women like that. You are so much more than them. You are sexy in a way that they could never be.'

Sexy. Suddenly Ana's self-consciousness drained away. Her mouth was dry. 'You do want me.'

He looked at her. Glared at her. She was filled with a fizzing, buoying sense of vindication.

'Ana...dammit.' He stopped. 'I won't lie to you. Yes, I want you. I'd have to be devoid of all my senses not to want you. But it's not happening.'

The fizzing deflated a little.

'It's because I'm a virgin, isn't it? I know you're much more experienced...that it takes threesomes to engage your interest—and I can't offer you that. Well certainly not here... There's only us on the island—'

'Whoa, wait—what? Threesomes?'

Ana shut her mouth. She was babbling.

Caio was looking at her as if she had two heads. 'What are you talking about?'

A wave of embarrassed heat rose up from her toes to her face. 'There was a piece online...about you and two supermodels...'

Another look of disgust flashed across Caio's handsome features. 'They put that story out there because I declined their very *un*-tempting offer to have them both pleasure me simultaneously. They were trying to boost their profiles. The piece disappeared once my legal team threatened to sue for defamation.'

'Oh...' Ana's voice was small. But she couldn't stop the small burst of relief she felt in her solar plexus to hear that he wasn't into performative sexual situations. Talk about intimidating...

'"Oh", indeed,' Caio said. Then, 'Look, there's no point making things complicated. We've got one night together and then we get on with our lives.'

Ana folded her arms across her chest. 'That's precisely my point. It doesn't have to be complicated.'

'Ana, look, it's not that simple. You're not experienced—'

'And I won't ever be experienced with that kind of attitude.'

Caio's eyes flashed. 'I will not be your first lover. I'm not the kind of man who is anyone's first lover. I'm not kind, considerate, gentle... and that's what you deserve.'

I don't want kind and considerate! Ana almost growled out loud.

'That's ridiculous,' she said instead. 'You were inexperienced once. You must have slept with a virgin before.'

Caio shook his head. 'Never. I'm not interested in that kind of emotional responsibility. In case it's escaped your notice I signed up to a marriage of convenience purely to avoid emotional investment. To focus on business.'

Ana recognised the obdurate look on Caio's face. She sat back down on the lounger and shrugged lightly. 'Fine.'

His expression went from obdurate to suspicious. 'Fine...?'

Ana sat back and stretched her legs out. She closed her eyes, crossing one ankle over the other. 'I'm not going to beg, Caio. I'll fix something for dinner around six p.m., okay?'

He said nothing for a moment, and then, 'Okay. See you then.'

Ana kept her eyes closed until she was sure Caio had gone back up to the villa. Then she opened them. *Fine*? No, it was not fine. She sat up straight. The memory of that night a month previously at the cancer charity benefit was still vivid. It was the night she'd worn that red dress. The one she'd felt sexy in. The one she'd hoped would provoke a reaction from Caio.

Except he'd been stony-faced and tense all night. Literally almost flinching if she touched him.

They'd actually left the event early, and hadn't exchanged a word on the way home, when usually they would chat idly about the people they'd met, or Caio would ask her what her opinion was of certain people or conversations they'd had.

When they'd reached the apartment he'd disappeared into his study. She'd assumed that it was because, contrary to turning him on, she was actively turning him off. And that with every effort on her part to make him notice her she was only driving him further away.

But it hadn't been that. It had been because she *had* been getting to him. He just hadn't wanted to admit it or act on it.

She'd hadn't fully acknowledged until now how rejected she'd felt that night. And hurt. Because over the previous months it had really felt as if they'd become a unit—not a conventional one, granted, but a unit. Supportive. Respectful. Almost…friends.

But since that night last month they'd been

careful to avoid each other. Ana had felt humiliated to think that she'd actually hoped Caio might find her attractive. That she'd put so much effort into transforming herself into a sleeker version of herself when she'd never had a hope.

That was why she'd booked a one-way ticket to Europe for the day of their divorce. She'd wanted to leave Rio ASAP and put Caio and her humiliating crush behind her.

But now everything had just flipped one hundred and eighty degrees.

Caio wanted her.

She was a complete novice in more ways than one, and especially when it came to the art of seduction. But he wanted her. That was all she needed to know.

CHAPTER ELEVEN

CAIO PACED BACK and forth in the den, with the French doors open and leading out to the opposite side of the garden to where Ana was.

She wanted him.

And she knew he wanted her. For a man who'd never held back from pursuing a woman he wanted before, this was novel territory. Up until now there'd been an unspoken agreement between them not to rock the boat. As soon as she'd appeared in that excuse for a swimsuit the boat had started to sink in choppy waters.

But he assured himself he was doing her a favour by not indulging in this mutual lust. He might not have slept with a virgin, but he'd been one once. And he'd learnt a valuable lesson at his first lover's hands.

He'd momentarily confused sex with emotion after that first experience with an older woman. He'd blurted out afterwards, 'I want to see you again.'

She'd turned around and looked at him with pity and said, 'No, you don't. You think you do, but this is just sex, *carinho*, you'll soon learn…don't worry.'

And she'd left.

He'd felt as if his heart had been cut out of his chest. But she'd been right, of course. He had soon learnt, and he hadn't made the same mistake again.

He wasn't about to subject Ana to a similar devastating revelation. Not after they'd spent a year together, getting to know one another and developing a mutual level of trust. In a way, she was the first real friend he'd ever had, and this was something he was only really appreciating now—how entwined their lives had become without him even realising it.

He thought back to when they'd returned to Rio de Janeiro after their tour through Europe. Next, they'd been headed to North America. But for a few weeks Caio had caught up with business in Rio. He'd got used to coming home in the evenings and finding Ana cooking, not realising at the time that she'd cooked the food herself from scratch.

For a man who was allergic to any notion of domesticity he'd found it surprisingly appealing, and they'd settled into a routine of sharing dinner and chatting about inconsequential things. They'd watch a movie together, or a documentary, both of them sharing similar interests—which Caio had subsequently blamed for lulling him into a false sense of security.

One day Caio had found himself postponing a meeting so he could get back to the apartment in time for dinner and he'd gone cold inside. At what point had they crossed some invisible line to turn this marriage of convenience into something that had begun to resemble a real marriage?

Boundaries had already been crossed. He wasn't about to cross the final one now. No matter what she did to provoke him. He could resist. He had the benefit of experience and wisdom gained from painful experience.

'What are you making?'

Ana was careful not to show her reaction to Caio's reappearance. She hadn't seen him since she'd been on the lounger. Admittedly, once the adrenalin had worn off, she'd enjoyed a couple of tranquil hours dozing and swimming and reading.

She'd returned to the villa to put on a thigh-skimming sundress after peeling off the swimsuit. So much for enflaming Caio to the point that he couldn't help himself. But she hadn't lost heart. Not yet.

She looked up, feigning surprise. 'Oh, there you are. If we weren't on an island, I might have suspected you'd left.'

He made a face. 'I was in the study, looking up some news sites to see if there's any mention of us or the kidnappers.'

Ana's hand stilled. For a moment she'd forgotten about the outside world. This island was like a bubble. 'Is there?'

Caio shook his head. 'No, nothing. I can't make any calls or send any electronic messages in case they're intercepted. We just have to hope that things are going according to plan for the security team. So...' he said.'What are we having?'

Ana continued stirring the sauce. 'Chicken in a white wine sauce with some fresh vegetables.'

'Sounds good. I'm going to take a shower...'

Caio turned and left the kitchen and Ana watched him go, her eyes on his tall, rangy body. Broad shoulders tapering down to slim hips, tight buttocks and long legs. In many ways he was still an enigma, even though she felt as if she'd got to know him on a level that most others didn't. Due to sheer proximity for a year. You couldn't help but pick stuff up—habits, behaviours—after spending so much time travelling together and sharing a living space.

The only thing they hadn't done was share a bedroom. *Yet*.

'Wait!' she called out just as he was disappearing.

He stopped and turned around.

She said, as nonchalantly as she could, 'I thought we'd make a bit of an effort tonight.'

'Effort?'

'It'll be our last dinner together.'

'Are you expecting me to wear black-tie?'

The thought of him in a tuxedo, even though she'd seen him in one hundreds of times, made her heart pump. 'You don't have to go that far.'

He shrugged. 'Okay.'

When Caio had disappeared, Ana stopped stirring and took a breath at the thought of staging a grand seduction. She considered not going through with it. Did she really want to try and fail to entice one of Rio's most renowned lovers? But something stubborn within her refused to give in. To admit defeat before she'd even tried.

Before she could lose her nerve, she finished preparing the food and then took off the apron and went up the stairs to her bedroom suite. She took a shower herself, luxuriating

in the powerful spray and steam, liberally ap-
plying the very expensive-smelling soap.

When she was out, wrapped in a towel, she
surveyed the clothes. The deep shimmering
royal blue dress caught her eye. She reached
out but didn't touch it, suddenly filled with a
sense that if she wore it she would never get
over the humiliation of rejection. Instead, she
pulled out a dress in a dark golden colour. Off
the shoulder, it hugged her body all the way
down to below her knee. It was sexy, but understated. After appearing all but naked in
front of Caio earlier, she wanted to aim for
sophisticated elegance this time.

She dried her hair—so much easier now
that it was about twelve inches shorter than it
had been—and put on a light layer of make-
up. She still wasn't overly confident doing her
own make-up, but she pushed aside her insecurities.

After putting on a pair of strappy gold sandals, she took a deep breath and went back
down to the kitchen. There was no sign of
Caio and she felt ridiculously nervous. She put
the apron back on over her head and went to
check the chicken in the pan and start cooking the vegetables.

She took out a chilled bottle of white wine
and two glasses—which she almost dropped

onto the tiled floor when she looked up and saw Caio standing in the doorway, wearing not quite a full tuxedo but a black suit and a white shirt, open at the neck.

His hair was damp. She could smell his scent from a few feet away, spicy and earthy. Masculine. *Deus*. She was like an animal in heat.

'Need a hand?' he asked.

She held out the bottle and glasses for fear she would drop them. 'Open the wine, please? The table is set out on the terrace. The food won't be long.'

She was aware of Caio finding a bottle opener and pulling the cork. Carrying the bottle and glasses outside. When the food was ready, she took off the apron and arranged the chicken and vegetables on two plates, then carried them outside to the table, aware of Caio's eyes on her. The balmy sea breeze skated over her bare shoulders and she could feel her nipples getting hard under the stretchy material of the dress.

He said, 'This looks amazing. Your skill with cooking really is a testament to how much you dislike your father.'

Ana retorted, 'You should see my *boeuf bourguignon*.'

The minute the words were out of her mouth

she realised that Caio would never see it or taste it. The sudden reminder of impending loss was like a knife between her ribs. But he was right—this wasn't about emotion. She'd come to respect him and trust him. That was all. Nothing more. Apart from epic levels of lust and desire.

Tonight was it. No fear. No regrets.

She was sorry she hadn't gone all out and worn the blue silk dress now. At least if she was going down, it would be in style.

She sat down and Caio handed her a glass of wine. She saluted him before taking a sip, relishing the crisp, dry taste that exploded on her taste buds.

He took a bite of the chicken and made a sound that connected directly with Ana's lower body, sending a wave of heat right through her core. Great. Now her appetite had fled. For food.

'Good?'

'Delicious.'

Ana forced herself to eat, barely noticing the way the succulent creamy chicken almost melted on her tongue. When she'd swallowed, she said, 'I was thinking earlier that it must be amazing here when there's a storm.'

Caio sat back and looked around. The sound of waves lapping against the beach could be heard in the distance. 'Yes, it would be. It's so exposed.'

Like she'd been earlier. Except she refused to feel embarrassed about that.

Caio ate some more and then asked, 'So what's your plan when you get to Europe? Are you going to apply to university? You should, you know.'

Ana felt insecurity rise. 'I'm not sure. I'll stay in Amsterdam for a while with Francisco and maybe get a job.'

'You don't need to work.'

Ana gave Caio a look. 'Do you really see me settling for a leisurely life of shopping and coffee mornings? I loathe shopping, and I never did fit into the socialite crowd.' She held up her neatly manicured hand to demonstrate. 'I never got false nails. If that's not proof, I don't know what is.'

'You're too intelligent for shallow chit-chat and false nails.'

A burst of pleasure caught at Ana's chest. 'Well, I don't know about that...'

'I do,' Caio said, pouring himself more wine and topping up her glass. 'You were always more interested in the conversations that were meant to exclude you and not remotely interested in the conversations that were meant to include you.'

Ana rolled her eyes. 'It's all so sexist and boring. Why do the women have to talk about the latest social events and who is marrying who and who's having a baby and who's not and who's getting divorced...?'

'We got divorced.'

There was an edge to Caio's voice. Maybe to remind Ana of the status quo and to leave it alone?

She decided to ignore it. 'Maybe they're talking about us now.'

'I've no doubt they are.'

'I mean, it wasn't exactly a secret that ours wasn't a love match.'

Caio made a snorting sound. 'Apart from our island hosts—who, I will agree, seem to have pulled off the urban myth of a happy marriage—none of those marriages are love matches. They're all business transactions.'

Ana looked at Caio. 'Did your marriage to me bring you the business dividends you wanted?'

His gaze narrowed on her, as if suspicious of her motives. She felt reckless again.

'It certainly did. It gave me the sheen of respectability I needed to expand globally and, in turn, I think you'll agree that it's given you your freedom. And your brother's.'

Ana lifted her glass. 'Yes, it has. But maybe

my freedom isn't all that I want. Maybe I want more.'

Caio tensed. 'Ana…' he said warningly.

She neatly deflected whatever he was going to say by standing up and saying, 'Dessert? Coffee?'

She needed coffee to counteract the way the wine was making her feel languorous. She needed all her wits about her.

'Sure,' Caio said, his gaze still narrowed on her.

Ana took their plates into the kitchen and prepared a tray with two small strong coffees and two perfectly prepared *brigadeiros*—a traditional chocolate sweet that both she and Caio loved.

She brought the tray out and handed Caio his coffee and one of the sweets.

She sat down and he surprised her by saying, 'Thank you for dinner. It was a nice idea to celebrate our last evening together. I wish you well, no matter what you decide to do, Ana.'

Now Ana looked at Caio suspiciously. He sounded utterly urbane. Reasonable. Telling her without telling her that he had no intention of muddying the waters of their last night together.

She lifted her coffee towards him in a salute. *'Saúde.'* The coffee was tart—the perfect accompaniment to the sweet. She sat back in her chair and looked at Caio. 'You asked me what my plan is when I get to Europe... Actually, I know the first thing I want to do.'

'What's that?' Caio took a sip of coffee.

'Lose my virginity.'

Caio choked on his coffee. Ana pretended not to notice. She lifted a shoulder. A bare shoulder. And said, as innocently as she could, 'Well, if you're not interested then I need you to tell me all I need to know about finding the right person. I'd prefer to avoid a bad experience, if I can.'

CHAPTER TWELVE

CAIO STRUGGLED TO get his breath back after Ana's bombshell. *'Well, if you're not interested... I need you to tell me all I need to know...'* That was pretty much all he'd heard.

Not interested? *Madre de Deus*, it was all he could think about. Peeling that dress off Ana's supple body and feasting on her bare flesh until she was flushed and pliant, begging him to sheath himself inside her...

He shifted in his seat, glad of the table that hid his body's rampant response since he'd seen her in that dress, clinging to every curve and line of her body.

She'd never looked more alluring than she did right now, and it made him think of that evening in London when she'd appeared before him, hair chopped and transformed into a vision of beauty that had short-circuited his thought processes for long seconds.

Up until that moment she'd effectively hidden herself from scrutiny, with her long hair and by choosing clothes that didn't flatter her shape. Caio had put it down to lack of confidence, and perhaps the influence of growing up without a mother figure or sisters.

The first time he'd actually seen the shape of her had been on their wedding day, when she'd come to him dressed head to toe in lace, like a bride from the last century. But that night in London she'd been in a slip of a black cocktail dress that had looked as if it was defying gravity, clinging to her chest and thighs, and Caio's first reaction had been one of a man from the last century. He'd wanted to tell her to change immediately into what she usually wore—the kind of clothes that had helped him maintain the illusion that she wasn't as beautiful as she was.

She had the kind of beauty that crept up on you and slapped you across the face for underestimating it. And he'd been as stunned as if someone had slapped him. But then he'd realised that his reaction was ridiculous. Told himself he should be embracing the fact that his wife had discovered her inner style and beauty maven. Her face had been revealed, its spectacular bone structure no longer hidden by a fall of silky hair. Eyes huge. Mouth…

Caio had said something to her then. He

couldn't even remember what. He'd just had to get them out of there before she saw her effect on him.

But then he'd started noticing men noticing her. And the women, sensing a rival. It had made him feel protective and...possessive. *Jealous*. Yet he'd managed to keep a lid on his control—mainly by focusing on work to the extent that he was too exhausted to think about much else.

But now control was just a word...and Caio wasn't sure if he even understood the meaning of it any more.

Ana suddenly stood up, and Caio had to fight to keep his gaze up. She said, 'Actually, there's a dress... I'd like your opinion on whether or not it'd be suitable for a date...'

'Ana—'

But she'd turned and gone back inside, disappearing before Caio could stop her. He gulped back the last of his coffee, but it wasn't helping the itchy feeling under his skin or the fire in his blood.

He stood up, restless. The sunset had somehow come and gone unnoticed and dusk was falling, bathing the grounds in a lavender hue. The birdsong of the night was starting up. It was an idyllic scenario, if only Caio could feel relaxed enough to appreciate it.

Right now, he knew he'd only feel relaxed again when Ana was on a plane and there was some serious mileage between them. Although, much to his chagrin, he wasn't even sure if that would do it. She'd embedded herself under his skin and in his blood so indelibly that he feared there was only one way to exorcise her...

Disgusted with himself, and wondering uneasily what the hell Ana was up to, Caio shucked off his jacket and went into the study/library, where he'd noticed that Luca Fonseca had a drinks cabinet full of the kind of whiskey that had aged in a barrel over many, many years in an Irish distillery on the edges of a misty mountainous lake. Perfect.

He helped himself to a measure from a bottle that was already open and swallowed it in one. He'd hoped the heat might eclipse the other heat in his blood, but so far it didn't seem to be helping.

He'd told Ana on their wedding night that he didn't sleep with virgins, and no matter how alluring she was he would not be tempted. Their marriage might be over, but he knew instinctively that seducing Ana would bring about the kind of emotional complications he'd spent his life avoiding, after witnessing the emotional minefield of his own parents' marriage.

He would resist. He had to. They only had a few hours left. How hard could it be?

Caio had just poured another shot when he heard a sound behind him and turned around. Earlier, when Ana had appeared in the swimsuit, his first thought had been that he would never erase that image from his mind. Well, it had just been erased and replaced.

And now he had a second thought: *I'm a dead man.*

Ana faced Caio across the expanse of room with every cell in her body mustering up the last of her courage. She hadn't noticed it getting dark outside. The low light threw out a golden glow and put everything into shadow. Including Caio's expression. Maybe it was better that she couldn't see his reaction.

She'd changed into the blue silk dress, and the way it skimmed her body made her feel as if she could be naked. The deep vee cut between her breasts almost to her navel. The dress was pretty much backless.

She'd put her hair up in a haphazard bun in a bid to try and cool her flushed face and neck as much to be artful, and tendrils fell down around her face.

She only realised in that moment that she'd forgotten to put shoes on. She was barefoot, and the dress was pooling around her feet because it was too long for her.

Suddenly she was overcome with self-consciousness, and she was about to turn around and flee when Caio said in a strangled-sounding voice, 'What in God's name are you trying to do to me, woman?'

Ana went still. He sounded tortured. She took a step forward and suddenly Caio's face was revealed. It was stark with the same look she'd seen earlier by the pool, and it made her heart skip a beat and her pulse trip at the same time.

It looked like…hunger. The hunger she felt too.

Some of her confidence—admittedly blind confidence—came back. When she spoke her voice was husky with desire and nerves. 'I'm wondering if this is a bit over the top for a first date? When I go to seduce the man who will be my first kind and gentle lover?'

Caio made a sound halfway between a laugh and a snarl. 'I can guarantee you that if you wear that dress, the man won't be kind or gentle. He'll have one thing on his mind.'

Ana took another step into the room.

'Maybe that's a good thing. After all, for my first time I want it to be about just one thing.'

'Do not say it, Ana.'

She lifted her chin. 'Sex?'

Ana saw Caio's hand tighten so much around the glass he was holding that his knuckles turned white. A sense of exhilaration gripped her. She was getting to him.

She held out a hand. 'Can I have some of that, please?'

Caio seemed stricken, frozen in place. But after a few seconds he held the glass out and said, 'Be my guest. I'll pour another one.'

Ana took the glass from him, noticing how he was careful not to let their fingers touch. Even so, she felt the crackle of electricity between them.

This was so on.

Caio turned away to pour himself another glass and she could see the play of movement in his muscles under the thin material of his shirt. He turned around and she lifted her gaze.

Caio raised his glass and took a deep swallow. Ana took a more measured sip from her glass, a little thrill going through her at the knowledge that her lips were probably touching where Caio's had. The golden liquid slid down her throat all too easily, leaving an oaky aftertaste and the burn of alcohol.

'Why does it have to be me?' he asked.

Because I don't want anyone else to touch me for the first time.

It was a visceral, almost violent response. Deeply emotional on a level she hadn't allowed herself to acknowledge before. But it had to be Caio. The thought of leaving this place, of not having known his touch, was suddenly terrifying.

Not that she could articulate all of that to him. So she said, 'Because I know you. I trust you. And I want you.'

But Caio was as immovable as a statue. A trickle of ice went down Ana's back at the very real prospect that Caio's control was strong enough to withstand all her very rudimentary attempts to seduce him. She'd laid herself completely bare and now he was going to reject her.

The picture of her mother walking away without a backward glance swam into her mind's eye, along with the memory of rejection, and the pain of abandonment. Except this time, she'd set herself up for the spectacular fall.

Ana could have been a queen in that moment. She was so dignified. Caio was used to women being direct, but not in such an emotionally honest way. That took guts. He felt humbled by her.

And in that dress…

He felt his final wall of resistance crumbling to dust. But before he could articulate anything he saw her chin dip a little, and some of her bravado falter. She put the glass down on a table beside her and looked at him. He could see the way her expression was closing in. Becoming unreadable. Her body tensing.

'Look, Caio, I'm not going to beg you—you're probably right…this would be a mistake. Let's just forget about it, okay?'

She turned as if to leave, showing her bare back to Caio, her skin luminous in the soft light, the sensual curve of her spine giving her an air of vulnerability. A great roar of possessiveness rose inside him. Feral in its intensity. Maybe earlier he would have taken her cue and packed his lust away in ice, told himself it was for the best that she'd come to her senses, but it was too late now.

'Wait a minute.'

She stopped. But didn't turn around.

'You're giving up so easily?'

She turned now, eyes flashing. It sent another roar through Caio's blood. This woman was his and no one else's, and he would be the first to awaken her. The thought of another man touching her made him feel violent. How had he ever thought he could resist her?

'I'm not a masochist, Caio. I've made it clear I want you to be my first lover but I think you're just enjoying toying with me.'

He shook his head. 'Come here, Ana.'

'You come here.'

The bravado was back.

He put his glass down and crossed the distance between them. He had an awareness of just how petite she was up close. Bare feet. But underneath the bravado he could see uncertainty. It pierced through the fire in his blood to send something alien to his gut. A need to reassure.

He put a finger under her chin and tipped it up. 'Are you sure about this?'

She said nothing for a long moment and Caio's pulse tripped. A cold weight lodged in his gut. What if she was regretting her decision? What if she wanted to change her mind? What if she was toying with *him*?

Suddenly he felt exposed.

Even though it killed him, he said, 'Ana, of course it's okay if—'

She lifted up a hand and put a finger to his mouth. She shook her head. 'What I was going to say was, would you just shut up and kiss me? Please?'

CHAPTER THIRTEEN

ANA COULDN'T QUITE believe she'd said those words. Up close, Caio was a lot more intimidating. Had he always been so big? They'd spent time in close proximity during social events, but never like this…in an intimate setting. It felt illicit. His finger under her chin was their only physical contact, but their bodies were almost touching.

He looked serious. 'This is one night. Tomorrow we go our separate ways.'

She nodded. 'What happens on the island, stays on the island. I get it.'

She would have agreed to anything. She couldn't take her gaze off Caio's mouth. She was barely aware of his hands cupping her face, tilting it up even more. Every cell and nerve in her body vibrated with a fine-tuned awareness as Caio's head dipped and his mouth met hers. It was silk and steel all in one moment. Heat and fire.

For a breath, everything was suspended. And then, under subtle pressure from Caio, Ana opened her mouth and he took the kiss from heat and fire to white-hot incineration.

For a moment she couldn't cope with the rush of sensation. It was overwhelming. Desire pooled between her legs, making her pulse throb. Her breasts were pressed against Caio's chest and her hands gripped his arms tight, as if that might help her stay afloat.

Caio pulled away. Ana opened her eyes. She felt light-headed. Dizzy.

'Okay?'

She nodded. Her mouth felt swollen, even after just a few seconds.

'Just breathe, Ana. We'll take it slow... okay?'

A fire rushed through Ana. Not slow. Not now. She'd been waiting all year for this. Forever. 'Not slow. *Now.*'

She pressed her mouth to his jaw and found the buttons of his shirt, undoing them with clumsy fingers. She reached his mouth again, and even though she knew her moves were inexpert Caio made a little sound in his mouth and put his hands on her hips, drawing her close again.

She could feel the press of his arousal against her belly and it made the heat between her legs gush even more. Mouths clinging, she let him taste her so deeply she could barely think. She caught his tongue and nipped gently, delighting in how his hands tightened on her hips and then moved around, one hand cupping her buttocks, squeezing her through the slippery silk of the dress.

She'd opened the last button on his shirt. She pulled back and pushed his shirt open, her eyes widening on his broad and tautly muscled chest. It was a thing of divine masculine beauty. She lifted her hands and traced her fingers over his skin reverently. Explored a nipple. She wanted to taste it with her tongue, but was suddenly shy.

Caio shrugged off his shirt. He led Ana over to a chair and sat down, tugging her onto his lap. She fell into the cradle of his hips, grateful that she didn't have to stand on shaky legs any more. Heat and steel surrounded her. Caio's chest bare under her own skin. She looked at him hungrily. Couldn't believe this was happening.

She reached out and traced the firm line of his mouth with her finger. He caught it. She looked at him. He took her finger into his mouth. A skewer of need arrowed right down to her groin when she felt the sucking motion on her flesh, and she squirmed slightly on his lap. His eyes flared and suddenly Ana couldn't breathe. They were burning with golden fire.

He pulled her finger out. 'I want to see you.'

Ana whispered, 'Okay.'

Caio found the hook at the back of Ana's dress. He undid it and the silky material fell away from her chest to reveal her bare breasts. Suddenly self-conscious, she instinctively wanted to put an arm up to cover herself, but Caio stopped her.

'You're beautiful. I've dreamt of seeing you like this…bared for me…'

Ana's heart quickened. He'd wanted her too. They'd both wanted each other. It gave her a sense of urgency.

She leant forward and pressed her mouth to his again, an unknown emotion clutching at her chest. Caio's hand was on her bare back, and as they kissed his other hand explored her breast, circling and cupping her plump flesh, coming closer and closer to the straining hard tip of her nipple.

When his palm closed over her breast, she drew back sucking in a breath. Caio squeezed her flesh, trapping her nipple between two fingers. Then he took his hand away and bent his head towards her, blowing on her flesh lightly before surrounding that peak in moist heat. Sucking on her hard flesh.

Ana's hands were on his head, in his hair, gripping him. She was breathing fast, struggling to comprehend and deal with the sheer exquisite pleasure coursing through her entire body just from his mouth on her breast. She couldn't quite compute how such a simple act could feel so…life-changing.

He lifted his head and smiled. It was wicked. He knew exactly how he was making her feel. She scowled and put her hands on his shoulders, shifting her body so that she was straddling his lap, looking down at him.

Caio's hands went to her hips, holding her firm, and he took merciless advantage of his position to subject her other breast to the same torture. Ana's head fell back. She wasn't even aware that her hips were making small circling movements on Caio's lap, instinctively searching for a deeper connection. For *more*.

He pulled her dress up over her thighs and then slid a hand between them, his fingers finding her underwear and tugging it to one side.

Ana stopped moving. Her pulse was heavy and loud. She looked at Caio, caught in the beam of those molten gold eyes. His fingers explored between her legs, where the secret

folds of her flesh hid the extent of her desire...
but not for long. Caio opened her up and she
saw the flush of colour on his face when he
felt for himself how much she wanted him.
The heat of her lust made his fingers wet as he
massaged her flesh, stroking up and into her
in a rhythm that took her by surprise, especially when at the same time his thumb flicked
the solid nub of flesh where all her nerve- end-
ings were quivering and straining for release.

Ana's thighs gripped Caio's tight. She came
up to give him more room, her hands like
claws on his shoulders as she moved up and
down on his fingers, his hand, as he stroked
her to her first orgasm. She didn't even know
what was happening until she fell over an edge
she hadn't seen, falling down and down into a
spiral of such intense pleasure that she shook
in the aftermath, in awe.

She felt as if she should be embarrassed,
but actually, in that moment, she felt a very
strong sense of feminine power.

She collapsed forward onto Caio's chest, her
face in the crook of his neck. His hand was
still between them, on her pulsating sensitised
flesh. His other hand was on her back, moving up and down in a curiously tender gesture.

His hand stopped. He said, 'Did you never...?

I know you're innocent, but I thought you would have…'

Ana's belly contracted. Now she did feel embarrassed. She pulled back. Caio took his hand from between her legs. She shook her head, avoided his eye. 'No… I didn't… I was in a house surrounded by men. It didn't feel very private.'

Caio found her chin and tipped it up so she had to look at him. 'You're very responsive, *carinho.*'

'Is that a bad thing?'

Caio quirked a smile. 'No, it's something rare…it's a good thing.'

'But what about you? You didn't…' She felt a blush rising up over her bare skin.

Caio shook his head. For a second he looked as if he was in pain. 'Don't worry about me. But we're not going to continue here. Not for your first time.' Ana didn't want to move in case they broke the sensual spell. But Caio was saying, 'Wrap your arms around my neck.'

She did, and he stood up, pulling her legs around his waist. He walked her through the silent villa like that, and up the stairs and into his bedroom.

The doors were open, curtains fluttering in the warm breeze. But Ana barely noticed.

Caio placed her on the bed. Her dress was pulled down to her waist and ruched up to her thighs. She didn't care. She felt languorous and sated and lethargic. But as she watched Caio bring his hands to his trousers, open them and pull them down, taking his underwear with them, revealing his naked body, she suddenly didn't feel lethargic any more.

She came up on her elbows, mesmerised by that stiff column of flesh. She dragged her gaze up to Caio's face, suddenly feeling out of her depth. How could she pleasure a man like this, who had already experienced so much pleasure with women far more experienced than her?

'Caio… I don't know what to do… What if I can't…?' She trailed off as he moved over her on the bed, resting on his hands.

He said, 'You don't need to think about anything. Just lie back and let me show you how it's done, hmm?'

Ana collapsed back onto the bed, every cell in her body pulsating with fresh need and desire. Caio was enormous over her, a naked warrior, and right at that moment she was prepared to surrender everything to him.

CHAPTER FOURTEEN

CAIO HAD NEVER seen a more erotic sight. And he knew it had nothing to do with a year of sexual abstinence and everything to do with the woman laid out on the bed before him. There was no other woman for him at that moment, and he had the strangest sensation—before he pushed it way down—that there wouldn't be again.

Dark hair was spread around her head and her cheeks were flushed. Chest bared, her plump breasts pouted towards him, tempting him to taste her all over again. The curve of her waist and the flare of her hips made his fingers itch.

The blue silk still pooled around her body. Caio reached for that first, tugging it down and off. She lifted her hips towards him, and the sweet, musky scent of her desire caught him off guard for a moment.

When he'd explored her body, and found

how ready she was for him, it had taken all his restraint not to position her over his lap, free his body from its confinement and bury himself so deep he would find immediate relief. But the fact that she'd never orgasmed before had caught at him in a way he hadn't expected. Making him feel protective. Possessive.

Now all she wore was her underwear. A flimsy lace thong. Caio dispensed with it easily. The cluster of dark curls over her sex made his straining flesh even harder.

He came down on his knees by the bed and pushed her thighs apart, exposing her glistening folds. *Deus*. He wasn't even sure if he could indulge in this when his body was screaming for release. But he had to make sure she was ready.

Ana's head came up. 'Caio?'

He said, 'Shh…just lie back…trust me.'

She let her head drop back. He put his hands under her hips and tugged her easily towards him. She was so petite. So delicate. Yet strong. He'd felt the strength of her body in its climax, and he had to admit that he'd never really noticed another woman's climax so acutely before.

He pressed kisses along the inside of her thighs, his hands under her buttocks. He could feel her starting to tremble as they had an effect on her, saw her hands close into fists on the bed.

The scent of her was intoxicating. He lifted her a little towards him and blew on her heated flesh before placing his mouth there, licking his way to the centre of her body and that sensitive cluster of nerves that responded under his ministration. Her whole body tensed for a moment, before she let out a little hoarse cry and lifted her thighs, as if she needed to contain the pleasure ripping through her body.

He drew back. He was shaking with the need to sheath himself inside her. He was almost ready to do it. But Ana was looking at him with wide eyes, and he could see that she needed more, even after coming for a second time.

She was looking at him so hungrily he almost threw caution to the wind, for the first time in his life almost forgetting—but at the last second he remembered, and cursed softly.

'What is it?'

Caio stood up and went to the bathroom, 'Protection.'

He came back and unselfconsciously rolled the protective sheath along his length, even that motion almost tipping him over the edge. Ana was exactly as he'd left her. Her chest lifting up and down with her uneven breaths. Legs spread apart. Right at this moment he didn't know how he'd resisted her for so long.

A warning bell rang in his head. He did know, but he didn't want to think about it now, because they'd gone way past the point of no return.

He said gruffly, 'Move back a little.'

She did so, her breasts bouncing with the movement. Caio almost groaned aloud. She was going to kill him. He was sure of it. But he would die happy. He was sure of that too.

He came down over her, careful to shield her from his full weight. He said, 'It will hurt a little, but it should ease…'

'I'm okay…just…please, Caio…'

She bit her lip, and that small, innocent movement pushed him over the edge of his control. He came closer and took himself in his hand, placing his erection at the entrance of her body, where she was still slick and hot. And hopefully ready… Because it was taking a restraint he hadn't even known he had to go slowly.

Caio felt Ana's resistance when he breached her body, saw the momentary flash of discomfort on her face. He almost stopped, but she reached up for him and wrapped her legs around his hips. 'Don't stop, I'm okay. Please.'

Gritting his teeth against how insanely good it felt to sink into her tight embrace, Caio felt small beads of sweat on his brow as he buried himself inside her. They were both breathing harshly. And they hadn't even started. Caio pulled out again, and then eased back in, feeling Ana's body gradually loosen its tight grip, hearing her breathing grow faster as the timeless rhythm took over.

Ana's body was pliant around him. He could feel the sharp tips of her breasts against his chest. Usually when he made love to a woman he didn't lose himself completely. There was a part of him that stayed aloof. In control. All of that was gone here. Caio was only aware of the slick slide of his body in and out of Ana's, and the tension growing at the base of his spine as he fought to hold back until he felt her body climax around his.

Caio was almost on the verge of not being able to hold the rush of release when he felt Ana's back arch and an infinitesimal moment of stillness before her paroxysms of pleasure made her body contract powerfully around his, precipitating the strongest climax Caio had ever experienced.

Ana didn't know how long she'd been out. She only knew, as she slowly regained consciousness, that she would never forget the onrush of pleasure that had broken her apart into a million pieces and put her back together but in a new way.

She wasn't *her* any more. She'd been altered.

The orgasms Caio had unselfishly lavished upon her before they'd made love couldn't possibly have prepared her for the ultimate pinnacle of pleasure. So much pleasure. And he'd denied himself this for a whole year?

Ana became aware of movement. Sounds. Running water. She cracked open an eye. It was dark outside now. Low lights were burning in the room. The bed was empty.

And then Caio appeared in the doorway of the bathroom. There was a cloud of steam behind him. He was bare-chested and wearing a pair of sweatpants, slung low on his hips. Ana's over-sated body tingled in response, and she felt hot when she thought of how she'd wrapped her legs around him, begging him to go deeper, harder…

She'd become someone unrecognisable. Or the person she was meant to be. *With him.* Except all that was too late. It was over. It had never really started. This was just…an indulgence.

She pushed aside the sudden melancholy

that gripped her as Caio came over and sat down on the bed. Ana felt shy. Which was ridiculous.

'How are you feeling? Are you sore? I'm sorry... I tried to be gentle, but I'm afraid I—'

Ana sat up, pulling the sheet up over her chest. 'No, it was fine. It was...perfect. I had no idea it could be like that. I'm sure for you, though, it must have been a bit...boring.'

She let her hair swing forward, hiding her face a little. An old habit. Caio reached out and put it behind her ear in a gesture that made Ana's heart thump. She felt raw in this moment. Exposed. But she forced herself to look at him.

He took his hand down. 'It was not boring, *carinho*. Trust me.' He looked as if he was about to say more, but then he stood up abruptly and said, 'I've run you a bath. You'll be a little sore, and I think you bled a little.'

Now Ana was mortified. She lifted the sheet and looked down to see spots of blood. Her face burned. 'I'll change the sheets.'

'I'll take care of that. Come and take the bath before it gets cold.'

He handed Ana a robe and she let the sheet drop so she could slip her arms into it, moving from the bed and trying to be as blasé as possible, as if she did this all the time. She imagined Caio's regular lovers paraded around naked without a care.

She belted the robe and tried not to acknowledge how the thought of Caio's ex-lovers and future lovers made her feel.

The bathroom was fragrant with a mixture of musky rose and something much earthier and more masculine. The bath was luxurious and filled almost to the brim.

Ana closed the door slightly, her face burning anew when she spotted Caio stripping the sheet off the bed. She pulled her hair back and put it into a rough knot then let the robe drop to the floor and stepped into the bath, wincing a little as the hot water came into contact with sensitive muscles and the skin between her legs.

The hot, fragrant water seeped into her body and made her feel even more boneless. She wanted to run her hands over her body where Caio had touched her.

Licked her. Nipped at her flesh. Sucked her.

Ana groaned, and resisted the urge to bury her head under the water. She felt a pang to think of how Caio hadn't been in the bed when she'd woken. What had she expected? To be wrapped in his embrace and that he would be whispering sweet nothings in her ear? He'd made it abundantly clear that this was a purely physical thing. One night only.

Except the only problem was that Ana already knew once wouldn't be enough. Not nearly enough. They had one night. She would have to make the most of it.

CHAPTER FIFTEEN

CAIO STOOD IN the kitchen, at a loss for a second. He knew what the problem was. His brain hadn't started functioning normally again yet. Sex with Ana had literally fried his brain. Rewired it.

He'd never lost it so completely like that. To the point where he'd lost any semblance or illusion of control. So much so that when he'd managed to surface, and had extricated himself from Ana's embrace and when she hadn't woken, he'd spent long minutes just watching her.

Her lashes had been so dark and long on her cheek. Mouth swollen from his kisses. Marks on her pale skin from his hands, mouth, stubble.

Horrified at his reaction because he never usually mooned over lovers after sex, he'd left her sleeping on the bed and filled the bath. And now she was in the bath, and all he wanted to do was go up there, haul her out, and bury himself inside her all over again. And again.

He cursed himself. He should have listened to his instincts when they'd told him that touching Ana would not be like touching another woman.

But then he castigated himself for such a notion. He hadn't had sex in a year. He'd never slept with a virgin before. Those two things combined were bound to make it feel...different. *Amazing*.

He heard a noise from behind him and turned around to see Ana hovering in the doorway, looking endearingly uncertain and also sexy as hell in the thin robe now belted at her waist and falling to mid-thigh. Her hair was wavy from the steam. Need skewered through him like an arrow, straight to his groin, before he could stop it.

'Are you hungry?' he asked abruptly.

Ana blinked. 'Yes, starving.'

She blushed, obviously thinking of how that appetite had come about, and Caio had to avert his gaze for fear he'd lose any ability to be civilised.

'Sit down. I'll make us an omelette.'

Ana came in and perched on one of the tall chairs on the other side of the island, and watched Caio break eggs into a bowl. He never usually felt self-conscious under a woman's gaze, but he did now.

She said, 'I've never seen you cook anything before.'

Caio glanced at her, and to try and keep himself busy, and not touch her, he poured a glass of wine and pushed it towards her. She took a sip. He took a gulp from the glass he'd poured himself.

He said, 'My repertoire is severely limited. Eggs, I can manage, but nothing more complicated.'

'Why did you ever need to cook?'

'When I left home, I'm ashamed to admit that I suddenly realised my food wasn't going to be prepared daily by a chef. So for a couple of years I lived on variations of eggs and takeout and street food.'

'When you were building your business?'

He nodded.

Ana asked, 'Did you really have no support from your family?'

Caio shook his head. 'My father disinherited me the day I left. I'd betrayed the family code.'

'How did you survive?'

'At first, with difficulty. I had some savings—the money I'd made from doing coding work for a tech company who'd seen a project I'd done at high school. I lived on that, stayed in hostels…getting odd jobs here and there. In my free time I pursued my own work, gradually building it up enough to seek investment…and that's pretty much it.'

Ana made a snorting noise. 'A modest way of describing a journey that led you to inventing a way to pay for products online that is now the most used online payment system on the planet, and to becoming a self-made billionaire by the age of twenty-five.'

Caio poured the egg mixture into a hot pan and looked at Ana. His mother was the only member of his family who had ever acknowledged his achievement. It felt strange, hearing it told to him by someone who wasn't a potential investor or a woman trying to feign interest.

There was no need for games with Ana— apart from the stunt she'd pulled just a few hours ago, which had led to the most mind-blowing sex of his life…

He shook his head, as if he could dislodge that assertion. He'd had sex like that before… he was sure he had. Even if he couldn't quite remember where or with whom…

In a bid to divert his mind and his libido from dangerous territory, Caio put the cooked omelette under the grill for a couple of minutes and commented, 'I know your mother wasn't a part of your family for long…why did she leave?'

Ana put down her wine glass and it clattered a little against the marble of the countertop. She avoided Caio's eye. When she spoke her voice was clipped, unsentimental. 'She'd had enough of my father's controlling ways. She figured she'd done her duty and so she left. She's married again now, with no children to complicate things.'

Caio noted that she'd echoed his words from earlier. 'Do you ever see her?' he asked.

Ana shook her head and took a sip of wine. Caio noted the slight tremble in her hand and his insides clenched.

'That's why Francisco and I are so close,' she said. 'We only had each other. And then, once he revealed he was gay, I became even more protective of him.'

'You were his mother?'

Ana shrugged minutely. She glanced at Caio. 'I guess…in a way.'

Caio flicked off the grill and got some bread. He said, 'That's rough, not having your mother, but I admire her for doing what my mother didn't have the guts to do.'

Ana frowned. 'What do you mean?'

Caio put his hands on the countertop. He'd never told anyone about this. He suspected not even his brothers knew. He looked at Ana. 'My father is a tyrant, not unlike yours. He's also violent.'

Ana sucked in a breath. 'Earlier, when you tended my finger, you said something and I thought… Was he violent with you?'

'Casual stuff when me and my brothers were small—a clip around the ear, stuff like that. But once we got big enough he knew he had to curb his urges to lash out. But my mother…she was an easier target.'

Ana looked shocked.

Caio said, 'The day your father brought you to meet me, to discuss our marriage—'

Ana made a sound. 'That's a diplomatic way of putting it.'

Caio's mouth quirked, and then he grew serious again. 'I thought he was going to hit you when you stood up to him.'

'My father was never violent, but there was always the threat of it in the air. Especially once he found out about Francisco. But he never touched him.'

Caio said, 'The threat of violence can be almost as bad as the act… I managed to persuade my mother to leave with me after one incident. A bad one. She refused to go to the police. But at least she left. We went to a hotel. For one night. When I woke in the morning she was packed to go home. She said she couldn't do it. Couldn't walk away from the only life she knew. That she'd grown to love him in spite of their marriage being arranged and his behaviour. So she went back. But I never did.'

Ana said carefully, 'I think it took huge guts for her to leave, and maybe to go back too. Being a woman in that world is not the same as being a man. Maybe she really felt she had no other option.'

'Perhaps,' Caio conceded. 'I hadn't thought of it like that.'

'Because you're a man,' Ana pointed out dryly.

He made a face. Then, 'Whatever her reasoning, if that's what love is—something born out of something so dysfunctional—then I want no part of it.'

Ana went very still inside, watching as Caio took the omelette out from under the grill and divvied it up onto two plates with some crusty bread.

'If that's what love is...then I want no part of it.'

Suddenly, as if the last piece of a jigsaw

was slotting into place, Ana saw Caio as if for the first time. She truly understood him now. Understood his willingness to enter into a marriage of convenience. All to avoid any emotional connection or entanglement.

And she got it. She came from the same cynical, emotionally barren world. Her own mother had walked out on her sons and daughter to pursue her own happiness. Ana knew she would never get over the awful sense of abandonment, confusion and loss she'd felt watching her mother get into a car and drive away.

And yet a small part of her had stubbornly refused to wither and die. Her relationship with Francisco had proved to her that there was such a thing as unconditional love. Deep inside was still a tiny seed of hope that one day she would find a way to heal from that awful sense of loss by finding a love to prove that all was not cynical and barren. To prove that she wasn't worth abandoning.

Except she'd failed at the first hurdle. Because she knew something else now. Something she couldn't keep denying to herself. And maybe making love with Caio had forced it to the surface, leaving her no way to hide from it any more.

She loved him. She'd fallen in love with him

in fits and starts since the moment she'd laid eyes on him and had assumed the worst of him. *She loved him.* And after what had just happened… She knew no other man's touch would ever come close.

'Eat up while it's hot.'

Caio pushed a plate towards Ana. In spite of everything her stomach rumbled, reminding her of just how mortal she was. Seizing on the distraction from too-disturbing revelations, Ana took a bite of the fluffy tasty omelette and made a sound of appreciation. 'This is *good.*'

Caio affected nonchalance. 'I told you—eggs, I can manage.'

Ana's appetite battled with the huge ball of emotion expanding in her chest. In spite of the painful things they'd just been talking about she'd rarely seen this lighter side of Caio, and it was…intoxicating.

She took another sip of wine and a bite of omelette. They ate in companionable silence until Caio pushed his own plate away. He was looking at her intently. Ana swallowed, her appetite for food suddenly supplanted by another growing hunger.

'How are you feeling? Sore?' he asked.

Ana blushed. 'I'm fine. The bath was…nice. Thank you.' It had been thoughtful. As had his lovemaking. He'd been constantly making sure she was okay. Giving her two spectacular orgasms before showing her that they had only been the precursor to the main event.

If he'd been a careless lover, intent on finding his own pleasure, it would have made it easier to tell herself she was being ridiculous, that she was confusing emotions with sex... But he wasn't. And she wasn't. She was in so much trouble. But there was no going back now. She couldn't put the genie back in the bottle. And right now she didn't want to.

'That's good,' he said.

'What's good?'

Caio came around the island and swivelled her chair around so she was facing him. All she could see was his bare chest...remember how it had felt crushed to hers...

She looked up.

'That you're not too sore... Because we only have one night, and I have no intention of wasting it.'

CHAPTER SIXTEEN

'WE ONLY HAVE *one night, and I have no intention of wasting it...*' Ana looked up at Caio. Suddenly she felt fearful. She'd thought the same thing herself only moments before. She'd actively seduced Caio for this purpose. But now she had cold feet. She hadn't counted on how making love with him would break her open, exposing a deep seam of need and emotion.

She knew the smart thing to do would be to call a halt now. She would meet someone else who didn't make her feel so...raw. *Wouldn't she?* she wondered a little desperately.

But she knew it was too late for that. This night would ruin her—*was* ruining her—for anyone else. And yet she also knew that she couldn't resist what Caio was offering. For one night only she would gather up these precious pieces of experience and pleasure so she could hold on to them like a miser.

He reached for her robe and opened the belt. Ana's breath quickened. She was totally naked underneath. He pulled the robe apart, baring her. Her skin prickled under his gaze, nipples tightening into stiff little buds.

She could see the pronounced bulge under his sweatpants and wanted to explore him, but before she could do anything so bold Caio lifted her wine glass and held it close to her breast, before tipping it slowly so that a trickle went over her breast and nipple.

She gasped at the cold sensation against her warm skin. Caio cupped her breast and bent down, his hot mouth closing over the peak as he sucked and licked her flesh clean of the sweet drink.

Ana was clutching his head, biting her lip to stop crying out, even though no one would hear them.

Caio pulled back and stood up, eyes dark and golden. 'I want you…'

Emboldened by the evidence of how much he wanted her, and wanting to seize as much of this night and experience as she could, Ana slipped off the chair, her legs feeling distinctly wobbly. She got down on her knees before him and put her hands to his pants, where they hung low on his slim hips.

Immediately she saw the flare of desire in

his eyes, even as he put out a hand and said, 'Ana, wait…you don't have to—'

'I want to.'

She curled her fingers under the edge of the material and slowly pulled the pants down. They caught for a moment on Caio's erection, and then it was free. Thrusting from the thicket of hair at its base. Boldly masculine and potent.

Ana was fascinated. Veins ran along the underside of the shaft and moisture beaded at the tip. She put a thumb to the bead of moisture and then licked it. The essence of Caio. Obeying some instinct she'd never possessed before, Ana wrapped a hand around Caio's length. It felt hot under her palm and fingers, the skin silky, slipping over the steely hardness underneath.

She looked up at him, and the tortured look on his face, stark with need, made her feel invincible. She hardly heard his sharp intake of breath when she put her mouth around him, exploring intently, tasting every inch of him.

His hands were in her hair and his hips started to jerk, and then he took his hands from her and before she knew what was happening pulled her up. He looked wild. He lifted her into his arms before she could protest, kicking his pants aside, taking her upstairs and back into the bedroom.

Ana, sprawled on the newly made-up bed, looked up at Caio as he stroked protection onto his length. It was still wet from her mouth, and for a second she lamented that she wouldn't feel him skin on skin—but all that was forgotten, and she sucked in a deep breath as he seated himself inside her in one smooth, fluid and devastating movement.

'Okay?' he said gruffly.

Ana nodded and gripped his arms. 'Make love to me, Caio.'

He did, slow and deliberate, taking her to the edge over and over again, delaying the rush of pleasure, until she'd wrapped her legs around him and was begging, 'Please, Caio... I can't take it...'

'Okay, *amada*, get ready...'

And then he drew out, before seating himself so deeply again that Ana was instantly engulfed in wave after wave of pleasure so intense that she almost regretted begging for release. Because this much pleasure... No one could withstand it.

Caio was still moving, seeking his own climax, sending Ana hurtling over the edge again as he stiffened against her and came, **his big body jerking against hers for a long** moment until, at last, the storm passed and Ana slipped into a pleasure- induced coma, her inner muscles still clamping around Caio's body, deep inside hers.

In that moment, just before she slipped into blessed darkness, she felt a profound and deep sense of peace.

Caio knew he should move. Normally after making love to a woman he had a clawing and urgent need to put space between them. But the same instinct he'd felt after making love to Ana for the first time was back. And this time it was impossible to resist. Primarily because he wasn't sure he had any bones left in his body.

Ana was curled into his side, one leg thrown over his, her hand resting on his chest, fingers spread out. Soft breasts pressed against him. Her breath feathered over his skin, deep and even.

Caio's hand moved over hers, to lift it so he could move. But instead he felt his fingers curl around hers. A siren song was calling to him just to lie there, not to fight the bone-deep pleasure coursing through his veins and arteries like soporific nectar.

He didn't want to look at what had just happened and how amazing it had been. How unprecedented. How she'd taken him in her mouth like a sorceress and had almost tipped him over the edge there and then, exposing him for being weak. For not having the control to withstand the inexpert ministrations of a woman who had been a *virgin* up until a couple of hours previously!

She might have been inexpert, but her effect on Caio had been all too devastating…

Caio assured himself that this was different. Ana knew the score. She was starting a new life in Europe and he would get on with his life, capitalising on the fact that he was now globally renowned and vastly more successful than he had been a year ago. Ana had been good for business. She'd fulfilled her duty. And he'd given her what she wanted: safety and security for her beloved brother.

All in all, a very successful business deal. And now this—the explosive fulfilment of mutual desire. He would never wake at night again, aching to know what she would feel like underneath him…around him. Now he knew.

And yet as he slipped under the veil of darkness, unable to fight the pull, knowing that gave him no sense of peace. Only the prickling sensation that the more he had of her, the more he would want.

When Ana surfaced to some kind of consciousness she felt boiling hot. Gradually she opened her eyes and realised that she was plastered to Caio's chest, all but clinging on like a monkey, one leg thrown over him as if to stop him escaping.

Except she couldn't escape either—not that she even wanted to—because his arm was firmly and heavily around her, plastering her to his side. She held her breath in case she woke him, revelling in the sensation of all that heat and muscle and sinew under her skin.

But as if he could hear her thoughts Caio opened his eyes and zeroed in on Ana before she could even attempt to put some very necessary defences in place.

'Hi.'

'Hi.'

Such an innocuous word after a storm. Her voice was gravelly. Hoarse from shouting. Begging.

Ana buried her face in Caio's shoulder, but that only brought her mouth into contact with his skin. She resisted the urge to press kisses there. To lick him. Her face flamed when she thought of how she'd wantonly got on her knees before him and taken him into her mouth as if she did it all the time. As if it wasn't her first time.

'What?' Caio tipped her chin up.

Emotion, unbidden, caught at Ana. *She*

loved him. A man who oozed cynicism and self-reliance. Who didn't need anyone.

'Is it always like…this?' She hated herself for asking, for revealing her vulnerability, but too much had been stripped away. Literally.

Caio tensed under her. She was expecting him to say, *All the time, and actually usually it's better*, and she braced herself for humiliation. Exposure. But then he said, 'No. It's not. This is…rare.'

Ana pulled back marginally, dislodging Caio's arm. 'You've experienced this before?'

Caio pulled his arm free. 'No…of course not. Because each encounter is unique. But I know how overwhelming it is the first time.'

Ana took her leg down from where it was flung, far too close to an area of Caio's anatomy that fascinated her. She rested on an elbow. 'Tell me about your first time.'

Caio lay back and looked at the ceiling. Ana resisted the urge to let her eyes drift up and down his spectacular body. She felt the stirrings of a resurgence of desire. *Already.*

'It's really not that exciting.'

'Tell me anyway.'

Caio sighed. He looked at Ana, almost scowling. 'I don't do this, you know.'

'Do what? Talk?'

'Talk after sex.'

'Why?'

'Because it tends to send mixed messages.'

'Such as that you might actually like a woman you slept with?' Ana tried to hide an amused smile.

'Something like that.'

'You don't have to worry about me getting mixed messages—after all, I practically had to hit you over the head and drag you up to my lair to make love to me, so it's not as if I'm under any illusions.'

She said the words lightly enough, but they felt heavy in her gut.

Before he could respond to that, Ana said quickly, 'Anyway—your first time. What was it like?'

'Mind-blowing.'

Ana immediately hated his first lover with a passion that scared her.

Caio said dryly, 'But you have to remember that men are simple creatures. It wouldn't have taken an awful lot to blow my mind at sixteen years old.'

Ana felt marginally mollified. 'Who was she?'

'A friend of one of my brother's girlfriends. She'd come to a party. She was older than me. I think she'd have preferred to be with one of my older brothers, but he wasn't interested. She found me lurking in a corner, watching the party, and took me to a private space and…initiated me.' He continued with a thread of self-disgust in his voice. 'The worst thing was that afterwards I was so awed and pathetically grateful. I thought I loved her. I followed her and told her I wanted to see her again. She humiliated me.'

Ana's hatred at the thought of his first lover turned to pity. She said, 'That wasn't nice.'

'No, it wasn't. But she did me a favour, really. She could have strung me along and made a much bigger fool of me than she did. I learnt my lesson early.'

'What lesson was that?'

But Ana already knew.

Caio turned and looked straight at her. 'Not to confuse sex with love.'

Ana opened her eyes wide and sat up, clutching the sheet to her chest. She made her lips tremble a little, 'You mean, you don't love me now, Caio? But what we just did…what just happened…it was so special—'

Caio moved so fast she didn't have time to think or speak. She was pinned under his big body, one leg between hers, another part of his anatomy stirring back to virile life, and he said, 'Very funny. I was a young, nerdy and naïve sixteen-year-old. You know a lot more than I did.'

Ana moved against him suggestively and wound her arms around his neck. 'I'm not sure I entirely grasp the concept—I think you need to show me again.'

Caio didn't need any encouragement. His mouth claimed hers with a ferocity that almost blanked her brain, but not quite. Because she knew she might have fooled Caio into believing that she was more savvy than he'd been at sixteen, and that she wouldn't be so naïve as to confuse sex with emotion, but she hadn't fooled herself.

CHAPTER SEVENTEEN

WHEN ANA WOKE AGAIN, she was alone in the bed. It was still dark outside, which added to the sense of timelessness and also comforted her. It made her think of Romeo and Juliet, and Juliet's insistence that it was the nightingale they heard as dawn approached after their night together, and not the lark.

Ana scowled at herself. She wasn't usually given to flights of literary fancy, no matter how much she wanted to go to England and study literature.

She stretched luxuriously, revelling in all the new aches and twinges in her body…the tenderness between her legs. She felt decadent, and she focused on that rather than anything more emotional.

There was no sound from the bathroom, so she slipped into the robe on the floor and went in search of Caio, not really caring if she seemed needy. They had one night and she wanted him again.

Forever. She blanked that thought out.

All was quiet downstairs; the kitchen was empty. Then she heard a sound from the area of the study/library, where she'd confronted Caio in the blue dress. That felt like an aeon ago now. She felt like a different person.

She stopped in the doorway. Caio was standing much in the same place as he had been the last time. At the drinks cabinet with his back to her. Except his back was bare this time and he wore those sweatpants again. And, if she wasn't mistaken, she thought she could see the faint marks of her nails on his back.

He turned around. 'I tried not to wake you.'

I'm glad I woke.

Ana didn't say that. She just shrugged. 'I don't think you did. I woke and you were already gone.'

He held up a glass. 'Drink?'

'Sure.'

Ana sat down in a big chair and curled her legs underneath her, accepting the glass that Caio had had in his hand. He poured himself another.

She sniffed it, and the scent made her nose wrinkle and caught at the back of her throat.

She'd been too nervous previously to wonder what she was drinking. 'What is it?'

'The same as before—a very expensive Irish whiskey.'

Ana looked up. 'Won't Luca Fonseca mind?'

Caio tossed back the golden liquid in one gulp. 'I'll replace it.' He poured himself another shot and took a seat in a chair just a few feet away.

She arched a brow. 'We survived a year of marriage but now I'm driving you to drink?'

Caio looked at his ex-wife. She was driving him to something. A kind of insatiable insanity.

Even now, after the last time—after he'd been sure that he was done, that his body could not possibly take or generate more pleasure—all he could see was her, sitting in that chair looking so innocent, her legs tucked up under her delectable body.

The robe gaped slightly, showing a tantalising curve of breast. He didn't have to see the puckered nipple to imagine it and know how it would taste, stiffening into a hard bud against his tongue.

When he'd woken a short time before it had been to find himself entwined with Ana again. He'd looked out of the window and felt both perversely relieved and frustrated that there was no sign of the dawn.

He'd come down here to put some distance between them and try to drown out the ever-present hum of desire in his body with the burn of alcohol. It was as if a switch had been flicked and he couldn't switch it off again. For the first time since they'd arrived on the island he felt claustrophobic. But it was an inner claustrophobia. A sense of wanting to get away from himself. Irritating and disconcerting.

Ana, oblivious to the maelstrom happening inside Caio, took a sip of the liquid. She made a little face. 'It burns...and it's smoky. Earthy. I like it.'

'It's peaty, from the bogs.'

'I've never been to Ireland.'

'You can go now. Nothing stopping you.' *Deus.* He couldn't string a sentence together.

'Maybe I will.'

The thought of Ana going off to explore the world on her own suddenly made Caio feel a mixture of things. Rudderless, and also panicky.

'What are you going to do with your new-found freedom?' Ana asked, slicing through the heat in Caio's brain.

He frowned. 'Work.'

Ana rolled her eyes. 'Apart from that.'

Caio felt a bit stupid. What else was there besides work and the transient release of tension and frustration with a beautiful woman? Except that hadn't appealed for some time now. A year, to be precise. And after tonight... He didn't want to think about that...

Before he could formulate a response, Ana asked, 'Why didn't you just marry one of your lovers or a mistress? You wouldn't have had to deny yourself for a whole year.'

Caio welcomed the kind of talk that defused some of the heat in his blood. And a chance to remind Ana, in case she needed it, not to expect that this night meant anything more than the physical.

'Because I needed a marriage where there was no risk of emotional entanglement. A woman who understood the parameters. If I'd married a lover, no matter what I'd said, she would have hoped that it meant more... and no lover has lasted longer than a couple of weeks. I have a short attention span.'

Or he'd *had* a short attention span. Caio hated the suspicion that his brain had effectively been rewired in the last year. The past few hours.

'Why me?'

Caio shrugged, careful to keep his expression neutral, not wanting her to see that his decision to marry her had been born out of far more complicated reasons than he'd ever really acknowledged.

'Your father wanted to do a business deal.'

'So I was just an added bonus.'

Caio shook his head. 'An integral part. You came from the right kind of family...you understood—*understand*—our world. And once you knew what I expected of you I could see that you weren't averse to the idea.'

'No,' she conceded. 'Not when you explained what you needed.'

Ana raised her glass towards him. 'Here's to a business arrangement successfully executed.' Then she said, 'My father would have done the deal with you anyway, even if you hadn't married me.'

Caio shrugged. 'Perhaps. The truth is that he needed me more than I needed him.'

'I bet he hated that.'

Caio recalled the barely concealed aggression of Rodolfo Diaz. 'He'd done his research on me. He knew that my personal life was beginning to damage potential business prospects. He knew I wanted to expand globally. When he mentioned you, and the prospect of marriage, I couldn't help but consider that it **was serendipitous.**'

Ana smiled, but Caio could see it was brittle.

'And so the perfect sacrificial virgin was handed to you on a platter?'

Caio took a sip of his drink and shook his head, 'There was nothing sacrificial about you, Ana. You were in control of the situation the whole way. You stood up to your father that day…you angered him.'

Ana's eyes flashed at the memory. 'I *was* angry with him.'

'You put yourself in danger.'

Ana looked at Caio. 'I told you he was never violent…'

'I think you pushed him over a line that day. I saw it in him. Remember, I've seen it before.'

Ana frowned now. 'With your mother…?'

Caio nodded.

Ana shook her head. 'I don't think my father would have actually struck me…'

But even as Ana said those words it was all too easy to imagine a scenario where Caio had walked away from the deal and her father had lashed out for the first time. The longer she'd been single and in his house, the more of a burden she'd been.

But she hadn't been able to leave until she'd known Francisco would be safe.

Caio was grim. 'I saw it in him that day.'

Ana focused her attention on Caio again. She frowned. 'So are you saying you offered to marry me to protect me?'

Caio said nothing and Ana's words hung in the air. She'd meant them flippantly but now they felt heavy as their meaning struck home.

She untucked her legs and sat up straight. 'My God—that's it, isn't it? You married me out of some sense of duty. To protect me. Not because I was a suitable candidate, but because you pitied me. You saw me as a potential victim, like your mother. You couldn't save her, so you tried to save me. When you didn't even know me.'

Ana put down her glass in agitation as it sank in. She'd always harboured a very secret hope that somehow Caio had seen something in her that had compelled him to ask her to marry him. Fresh humiliation scored at her insides. Would she ever *not* feel humiliated on some level by this man?

'Ana, wait. It wasn't—'

But she stood up, cutting him off, not wanting to hear some platitude. It all made sense now. And she knew, after a year of living with him, that he had an ingrained sense of integrity and decency. He might have wanted her for what she could bring to the marriage, but he'd also wanted to save her.

She went to walk out, but Caio leaned forward and caught her hand. 'Ana, wait.'

She stopped. Even that small contact made lust surge. It was too new. Too raw. She pulled free and looked at him. He was sitting forward on the chair. His jaw was stubbled. Suddenly all her feelings for him were too jumbled to make sense of. Right now he looked like the louche playboy he'd been before they'd married, before he'd wanted to clean up his reputation.

All she'd done here tonight was allow him to scratch an itch before he went back out into the world a free man with a clear conscience—because she'd *begged* him to make love to her, to take her virginity, and also because he'd saved her from her father.

She felt sick.

Caio stood up. 'Ana—'

Panicked by the thought that he'd touch her and scramble her brain even more, she got out a strangled-sounding, 'No!' and fled from the room. Straight out into the garden.

It was lit up with solar-powered lanterns. She went blindly down towards the beach, attracted by the sound of the waves, needing to put space between her and Caio. It was clear and still, and the moonlight lit up the beach almost as brightly as if it was day. Ana sucked in a deep breath. She hated it that Caio had pitied her. She didn't want to evoke someone's sense of duty. She wanted to drive someone—*him*—mad with lust and passion.

And she thought she had.

But the truth was that it had taken a year for him to see her as a woman. To want her. And who was to say that his desire hadn't been fuelled by sexual frustration, compounded by being stuck on an island?

The past few hours, which had felt so wondrous and revelatory, now felt cheap.

She heard a sound behind her. She couldn't bear for Caio to see her vulnerability, so she turned around and pasted a smile on her face. 'Sorry, I went down a rabbit hole for a moment. I'm quite tired now... I'm going to bed.'

She went to walk past Caio, who was just a couple of feet away, and tried desperately not to notice his bare chest, or the way the sweatpants hung so precariously low on his hips.

'Ana, please. You have it all wrong—'

She put up her hand. She really didn't want to hear an explanation. 'It's fine, really. Look, we both know this was just a reaction to extreme circumstances, right? I wanted to get rid of the burden of my innocence before going to Europe, and you've taken the edge off a year of celibacy. We both got what we wanted.

We'll be out of here in a few hours. Hopefully. I need to get some rest now.'

Caio watched Ana walk back up to the villa in her short robe. He wanted to stop her and talk to her, but something held him back. His conscience. What could he say?

He turned around and emitted a curse. He hated that she'd come to the conclusion she had, but maybe it was for the best. She was right. In a few hours they would be leaving this place. They'd be moving on with their lives. No matter how good tonight had been… it was over now. It wouldn't help to go after her and try to articulate things he could hardly articulate to himself.

CHAPTER EIGHTEEN

AN HOUR LATER, Ana was still tossing and turning in the bed. After a lifetime of sleeping alone, she now felt the lack of Caio's body like a missing limb. Pathetic!

Angry with herself for allowing her emotions to control all logic, and for allowing herself to fall for someone who was so inappropriate for her, Ana got out of bed. In spite of very little sleep, she felt full of pent-up energy. And sexual frustration. Caio had awoken a need in her that she feared would never be assuaged.

The prospect of that made the sense of desperation even more acute. She needed to do something to defuse the turmoil and tension in her body. Usually she'd go for a run. Or a swim. She thought of the pool, but it was too... calm. She needed something more elemental.

Where the hell was she going?

Caio couldn't sleep, and was standing on

the small balcony outside his bedroom. He'd just been contemplating numbing the clamour in his head and the sexual frustration in his blood with more whiskey when a movement had caught his eye and he'd seen the slim shape of Ana, robe belted tightly around her waist, walking down the garden towards the beach—again.

Before he could stop himself, Caio went out to follow her.

When he got down to the beach, it took his eyes a minute to adjust. He couldn't see her. All he could see and hear was the pounding foam of the waves. And then he saw her discarded robe and a couple of other items. He picked them up. A delicate lacy top and matching pyjama bottoms.

It made him think of that moment when he'd come out of the shower into his bedroom—they'd been in some city...he couldn't remember which now—and he'd looked up to see Ana standing in the doorway, staring at his body as if she'd never seen a naked man before. Transfixed.

He'd known she was a virgin, but it hadn't really impacted on him until that moment just how innocent she was. And, if he was honest, that had been the moment when she'd burrowed under his skin and lodged herself there like a briar. He hadn't been able to get her huge eyes out of his head. How awed she'd looked. And then how mortified.

She'd never mentioned it. And neither had he. But a very subtle tension and awareness had come into the air between them after that night.

He looked out to the sea. He couldn't see anything. For a second he felt fear. Panic. She wouldn't possibly—? But then he saw the methodical stroke of arms in and out of the water as she swam parallel to the shore and relief made him feel like a fool.

Had he really considered that she was upset enough to do something drastic? When, as she'd told him herself, she was delighted to have been relieved of her virginity so she could go and enjoy her new solo life in Europe?

Caio's emotions swirled into a volatile mix, and without thinking about what he was doing he strode into the sea.

The first inkling Ana had that she wasn't alone was when she was unceremoniously hauled up by two big hands under her arms. She inadvertently swallowed sea water and spluttered, tried to clear her eyes, but of course it could only be one person. *Caio.*

When she saw him he looked fierce. His hair was wet, plastered to his head. Eyes burning. Ana realised she was standing up, the water waist-deep for her and up to Caio's thighs, where his sweats were moulded to his body.

He shouted, 'What the hell are you doing? You could have drowned out here on your own.'

Anger at him for making her *feel* so much, and for finding her in a private moment when she'd been seeking some peace, made her shout back. 'I'm perfectly safe! I'm a trained lifeguard and my brother and I used to go swimming in the sea regularly at night.'

'There's a perfectly good swimming pool here.'

'I wanted something more,' Ana lobbed back, feeling reckless. Feeling she had nothing to lose.

Dangerous.

'What if you'd got cramp? Or drifted out to sea?'

'I'm sure the security boats would have picked me up.'

'Ana... *Deus.*'

Caio let her go abruptly and Ana swayed against a wave. The current was dragging her back to shore. She was naked. As if he'd just registered that fact, Caio's gaze drifted down, over her breasts to her belly, where the water lapped against her skin. Back up.

'You regularly swim naked?'

'Not with my brother, no. But I figured I was safe here.'

'Unless you're giving the security men a show.'

Ana subjected him to an appraisal. 'Then we both are.'

His sweatpants were all but clinging to his hips, moulded to every taut muscle and one in particular. Even now, in the cold sea, he wanted her. Desire surged through Ana's lower body. She felt elemental. She wanted to punish Caio, except she couldn't remember for what, exactly.

A wave caught her at that moment and sent her off balance. She fell against Caio and he almost fell back too, grabbing her arms to steady her. Her breasts brushed his chest. Electricity crackled between them.

Without saying a word, Caio took Ana's hand and led her through the shallows and out of the sea to the beach. Still without words he let her go, and peeled off his sodden sweatpants.

They were both naked. Alone on this beach, on an island in the middle of the Atlantic Ocean. And suddenly nothing mattered. Nothing but forgetting about everything else but *this*.

Ana didn't know who moved first, but they were in each other's arms and their mouths were fused within seconds, tongues tasting and thrusting deep, hearts pounding.

Caio pulled Ana down so that he was on his back and she was straddling him. She needed him as she needed air to take her next breath.

Acting completely on instinct, she rose up and found him with her hand, positioned herself above him. Bracing herself with her hands on his wide chest, she slowly sank down onto his hard body. Caio's hands went to her hips and he let her dictate the pace as she got used to the sensation, rising up and down, until another more primal rhythm took over.

They were both wet, salty, covered in sand. Locked in their own intense storm. It gathered around them, growing and growing, until Caio held Ana's hips still so that he could pump up into her body.

She cried out and arched her back as ecstasy ripped through her and threw her high. The waves of pleasure were slowly receding when Caio pulled free from sensitive muscles and she felt the hot release of his own climax on her skin.

She collapsed onto his chest, spent. Skin hot...sticky. Her hair was wet. Caio's hand drifted up and down her back. Cupped her bottom.

One minute she'd been in the sea, letting the steady motion of swimming bring her back to some semblance of calm and equilibrium, and now...

Caio somehow managed to move them both and lifted Ana into his arms.

She protested weakly. 'I can walk, you know.'

'Shh...'

She spied the detritus of their clothing. 'Our clothes...'

'I'll get them later.'

Ana giggled. She felt drunk. 'What if they get washed out to sea and end up on Copacabana Beach?'

It felt so nice, being carried against Caio's chest, her arm looped around his neck. But then she saw something over Caio's shoulder, and the languorous heat in her blood cooled a little.

'What is it?' Caio's chest rumbled against her.

She shook her head and turned away. But it was too late. She'd already seen it. The faintest of pinks on the horizon. The dawn, heralding a new day. *The end.*

'Nothing, it's fine.'

But it wasn't fine. She didn't care about the revelations of before right now—she just cared about eking out as much time as she could with Caio.

She closed her eyes against the sight of oncoming reality and pressed her mouth to Caio's jaw. He was carrying her through the villa now, and up to his bathroom. He put her down and reached into the shower to turn it on, the space quickly filling with heat and steam.

He drew her in and she stood against the wall under the spray. She'd never felt so lax. So boneless.

Caio lathered up some shampoo and said, 'Close your eyes.'

She did. He turned her around so that she was facing the wall and put his hands in her hair, massaging and soaping the sea and the sand out of her hair. Her head fell back as he rinsed it away. Soapy suds sluiced down her body and she felt Caio move closer behind her. His erection pressed against her and she wanted to turn around. But an arm had snaked around her torso, holding her upright.

One hand found her breasts, massaging

and kneading, trapping her nipples between two fingers. Ana whimpered. His other hand went down, over her belly and over the curls between her legs, gently pushing her thighs apart so that he could find the slippery and hot centre of her desire.

Again. Already. Forever.

Ana made another noise as Caio's fingers delved deep into her sensitised muscles. It took only a couple of strokes for her to fall over the edge again, shuddering against him helplessly. Even as she thought she couldn't possibly take any more she knew that this was better than remembering what had upset her earlier.

Caio turned her around and she looked up at him. He was magnificent. A warrior. He lifted her so that she rested back against the wall and said, 'Hook your legs around me.'

She did so, and Caio held her safely, with awesome strength, as he stroked his way into her body. Skin on skin. It felt amazing. And just when Ana thought she couldn't possibly experience another ounce of pleasure, Caio proved her wrong.

It was fast and explosive. He pulled free of her body just as her muscles clamped tight around him, and he shouted out an unintelligible word as his own climax ripped through him. It was an awesome sight, to see this man's entire body convulse with pleasure as he held himself in his hand and allowed his essence to drain away.

Ana felt shell-shocked. Hollowed out.

Caio turned off the water and wrapped her in a towel, rubbing her dry and putting another towel around her head. He towelled himself dry and then took her into the bedroom. She fell onto the bed and fell into an instant dreamless sleep.

Caio watched Ana sleeping on the bed. He felt as if an earthquake had just ripped through his body, leaving nothing but rubble in its wake. He'd never experienced a night like this, when the minute after climax he'd wanted to take Ana again. And again.

He turned away from the bed and towards the French doors, which were open. He saw what she had seen. The dawn creeping over the horizon, bringing the new day with it. He saw the lights on the security boats bobbing on the water around the island.

It was over.

The rubble inside him turned to ash. Ana thought he'd married her out of an impulse to protect her because he hadn't been able to protect his own mother. And clearly that both-

ered her. He got it—no one wanted to be per-
ceived as a victim. But he didn't perceive her
as a victim at all. And he hadn't then.

But what he *had* felt wasn't worth mentioning, because it wouldn't amount to anything. Tonight had been…extraordinary. But it
was just sex. Mind-blowing sex. He and Ana
had had a business agreement for a year, and
they'd both got what they wanted out of it.

It was over.

CHAPTER NINETEEN

WHEN ANA WOKE this time it was bright outside. She could feel it against her eyelids and didn't want to open her eyes. But she had to. She squinted at the sunlight.

She was lying under a light cover, still with the towel wrapped around her. Caio must have unravelled the towel from her hair, and it was under her head on the pillow.

She was alone. She sensed a distinct change in the air. The spell of last night was broken. She felt it as keenly as a cool wind across her skin. In fact, if she hadn't been in Caio's bedroom, and if her body hadn't been aching all over, she might have fancied that she'd just spent a night with the most lurid dreams she'd ever had.

But it hadn't been a dream. It had been real. And epic and devastating all at once.

Not wanting Caio to find her lying there mooning, Ana got up and groaned when she saw the state of her hair in the mirror. She looked as if she'd been pulled through a bush backwards. She was relieved Caio wasn't witnessing this. As if he needed reminding that he'd be returning to more sleek and sophisticated lovers soon.

She pulled the towel tighter around herself and crept out of the bedroom and back to her own, closing the door softly behind her. She'd barely slept in her bed apart from that one sleepless hour before she'd decided to take a night-time swim in the sea and then Caio had appeared like an avenging sea god.

Ana groaned again when she thought of making love on the beach like two crazed teenagers. What must Caio think of her? Insatiable...wanton.

She had another shower in her own bathroom and tried not to notice the sensitive places on her body. The marks on her skin that told of big hands clasping her hips, holding her still so he could pump powerfully into her body.

When she got out, she dressed in loose black trousers and a dark red sleeveless silk V-neck top. Flat black shoes. She wanted to look mature. Elegant. Put-together. Nothing resembling the hot mess she felt inside.

She went downstairs and the kitchen was

empty. Ana breathed out a sigh of relief. She wasn't sure if she'd ever be ready to see Caio again after last night. But then she saw him. He was standing on the terrace dressed in jeans and a dark polo shirt, thick hair still damp from the shower.

He lifted his arm and Ana could see he was drinking from a small coffee cup. Her insides twisted. Something else they had in common. Strong coffee first thing in the morning.

As if sensing her regard, he turned around. He was clean-shaven. His face was carefully devoid of expression. Perhaps because she literally didn't provoke a reaction in him. Even after last night.

She forced a smile, as if this morning-after scenario wasn't going to kill her. 'Morning.'

He said, 'I made coffee. It's still fresh.'

'Cool.'

Brilliant, she'd regressed to being a teenager. She turned around before she could embarrass herself even more and went straight to the coffee machine, helping herself to a shot of thick dark coffee. The hot, rich liquid gave a much-needed shot of adrenalin to her veins.

Caio came in and stood on the other side of the island.

She held up the cup. 'That's good, thanks.'

'How are you feeling...after last night?'

She avoided Caio's eye. *Oh, God, he was going to be nice about it. Considerate.*

Feeling exposed, Ana asked a little waspishly, 'Do you normally ask your lovers how they're feeling the next day?'

'No, because I'm not usually around.'

'And now you feel compelled to because we're stuck on an island?'

'You were a virgin.'

Ana put down her coffee cup, its brief restorative effect turning to bile in her stomach. 'I think I'm probably more aware of that fact than you are, but thanks for the reminder.'

Caio cursed softly and ran a hand through his hair. 'Sorry... I didn't mean it like that.'

Ana said quickly, 'We really don't have to do this whole morning-after thing. I'm fine. Really.'

His voice sounded tight. 'Look, Ana, I wanted to talk to you about what you said last night... I never got a chance to explain, and I wasn't going to, but you deserve to know.'

Ana had picked up a piece of fruit, as much to look busy as to satisfy her non-existent appetite. She put it down again. 'You don't owe me an explanation.'

But he was insistent. 'I do. It's not fair for you to think that I married you because you reminded me of my mother. It was more complicated than that. I never saw you as weak or a victim, Ana. I married you for all the reasons I outlined, but also for another, much less tangible reason. An instinct. I cared what happened to you.'

'Which is just another way of saying you felt like you had to save me from my situation.'

Caio balled his hand into a fist on the kitchen island. 'Dammit, Ana—no, it's not. I'm no one's saviour. I knew that after my mother went back to my father. I just…saw something in you that transcended all the very concrete and practical reasons for marrying you. Maybe it was chemistry, which I wasn't prepared to admit I felt, because that would have complicated matters.'

Ana pushed down a dangerous bloom of hope. 'You don't have to pretend you fancied me all along to make me feel better, Caio. Please don't patronise me. I know last night was an aberration but, as I said, we both got something out of it and now we can get on with our lives.'

'You sound very…okay with everything.'

'Why shouldn't I be?' Ana forced some more coffee down her throat, hoping it would burn away the growing ache she felt at her core. The pain near her heart. This was ex-cruciating.

'Because last night was…intense.'

Ana affected a nonchalant shrug. 'I don't have anything to compare it to, but I'll take your word for it.'

Caio sounded grim. 'Believe me, it was not usual.'

Ana's heart thumped. 'Like I said, I'll just have to take your word for it.' A reckless devil inside her made her say, 'I can let you know once I've had some more…experiences.'

The colour in Caio's face grew darker and after a minute he got out a very terse-sound-ing, 'That won't be necessary.'

For a moment Caio looked almost tortured. Could it be possible that he was actually… jealous?

But before that flight of fancy could sweep Ana away there was a strident piercing noise. It was so unexpected that it took her a moment to identify it as the ringing of a mobile phone. Caio's phone. Which was now vibrating on the island between them.

Ana's guts turned to water. This was it. The outside world was back. What if they were told they had to stay for longer? That pros-pect alternately made her feel ridiculously re-lieved and also sick. Clearly Caio was ready to draw a line under the whole experience and move on.

He looked at her as he picked up the phone. He listened for a long moment and then said, 'Okay, that's good news. Thank you for all your hard work.' And then, after a few more seconds, 'Yes, we'll be ready. Thank you, Tomás.' He took the phone from his ear.

Ana couldn't speak. She just lifted a brow in query.

'It's over. They got the gang. They mounted a huge operation using two stand-ins for us. The gang had no idea we'd managed to escape. Security forces in Rio and Europe followed the stand-ins, and the gang were arrested in the act of kidnapping "you" at the airport in Amsterdam, and "me" in Rio. They didn't want to tell us how big the operation was until they knew it was successful, but it had been in the planning for some time before we heard about it.'

'Oh, wow.'

Ana felt flat. Somehow the fact that a major kidnap operation had been averted didn't have as much of an impact as the fact that they could now leave the island.

'They're sending a helicopter to get us; it'll be here within the hour.'

Within the hour.

A sense of panic, dangerous and far too exposing, rose like a ball from Ana's liquefied guts. But she just nodded her head and said, 'I should retrieve those clothes from the beach and pack.'

Caio put out a hand. 'No, I'll do it.'

But Ana was already walking out of the kitchen and down the lawn, in a bid to escape. She slipped off her shoes and left them on the grass, and stepped onto the beach in her bare feet.

She spotted Caio's sweats and her night clothes. They looked flimsy in the daytime, and she couldn't quite believe she'd felt compelled to come down here and swim in the dark. A moment of insanity induced by lust.

Caio was right. It had been reckless and dangerous. But she could remember the feeling of needing to connect with some elemental force. And now that elemental force was within her and she would never be the same.

She sensed Caio behind her. The suspicion that he wasn't remotely fazed by last night and the fact that they would be parting ways made her feel desperate, and also devastated. Now she could understand why he'd been reluctant to sleep with her—because he'd known better than her that she would find herself in emotional turmoil.

Except he had no idea that her turmoil had far deeper roots than merely confusing sex with emotion or because he was her first lover. He had no idea she'd been falling for him over the last year. That this was no overnight sensation.

He couldn't know. He couldn't possibly ever know how devastating this was for her. She'd already exposed herself so much by seducing him that this would kill her. And so, as he came alongside her, she affected an expression of bland neutrality.

CHAPTER TWENTY

A year ago, Cristo Redentor Church, Rio de Janeiro

ANA DIAZ WAS LATE. Approximately ten minutes late. Which was perfectly respectable—expected, even—on a traditional wedding day, but this wasn't a traditional wedding, and Caio could feel a prickling sensation at the back of his neck.

He was acutely aware of the small congregation behind him, whispering and looking at him. Speculating. A sense of exposure crept over him when he thought of the fact that Rodolfo Diaz was a notoriously tricky individual to do business with, and Caio had only done so because he'd known that Diaz had more to lose than he did in their deal.

But now he wondered if he'd missed something. If he'd got it wrong. Perhaps the marriage set-up with his daughter, Ana, was some sort of distraction technique—she'd stand him up at the altar, publicly humiliate him, and wreck Caio's reputation with a view to undermining his business. After all, Diaz knew his weak spots—hence the suggestion of a convenient marriage.

Caio imagined his father gloating. He'd always hated the fact that Caio had left the family and made a fortune all on his own. He'd love to see his youngest son fall flat on his face. And nowhere better than in the middle of high society in Rio de Janeiro.

But just as he was beginning to fear the worst he heard the congregation hush behind him. The surge of relief caught him off guard. He turned around to see Ana on her father's arm in the church's entrance.

She cut a curiously traditional figure, in a long dress that covered her from neck to toe and shoulder to wrist. A veil covered her face. But he could see her long dark hair, drawn back from her face.

She started walking down the aisle. For the first time Caio could appreciate her figure. She was usually wearing something baggy, making him wonder what she was hiding. But even in this less than fashionable wedding dress he could see that she'd been disguising a slimly petite figure with tantalising curves.

He imagined her long dark hair tumbling down her narrow back and a spark of desire made his blood pulse. He immediately tensed against it. This marriage was not about desire. It was about business, pure and simple.

She'd reached him now and he could see her eyes under the veil, huge and dark. Something about the modesty of her dress caught at him. He realised that after years of seeing women parade in front of him in as little as possible there was something erotic about Ana's entire body being covered up.

And then he had to grit his jaw and exert control again. He wouldn't be peeling this dress off his new wife.

She was looking up at him from under her veil and Caio lifted it up and over the back of her head, revealing her face. The purity of her bone structure and the lush natural pout of her mouth gave him a sense in that moment that he might very easily underestimate this woman, and that it would be a mistake to do so.

Then he noticed that she looked irritated. He said, for her ears only, 'Okay?'

She gestured minutely towards where her father stood to one side. 'I'm sorry I'm late. He delayed us…just to prove some macho point to you or something, I'm sure.'

So Caio had been right. Diaz might not have gone so far as to ruin the wedding, but he wasn't above playing games. He had never expected Ana to be in his corner with such a lack of guile. He felt a surprising sense of kinship with her. Even though he barely knew her.

He took her small hand in his and said, 'Let's do this, shall we?'

Now she looked nervous, but determined. 'Okay.' And she turned to face the priest.

It took a long second for Caio to take his eyes off her face and turn to the front...

The memory of their wedding day lingered in Caio's head. He'd thought of it because looking at Ana's profile now, as she stared out to sea, reminded him of that day in the church for some reason.

Her profile looked serene. He knew he should be feeling serene too. He'd just experienced a night of unexpected and unbridled passion and now he was a free man again. His business had never been better, nor his prospects as good.

But he didn't feel serene. He had the same feeling he did when he hadn't prepared well enough for a business meeting and knew he was at a disadvantage or on the back foot. The same feeling he'd had when he'd realised that he was in danger of eroding his success unless he did something drastic.

Marrying Ana had been a drastic move. But it had also been the best decision he'd ever made.

She looked totally impenetrable. Even though they'd spent a year together, and last night had effectively smashed aside the last boundaries of intimacy, right now he felt as if he knew nothing about her. She was as much of a mystery as she'd been when they'd first married.

'What are you thinking about?' The fact that he'd had to ask that question because she wasn't simpering all over him irritated Caio.

Ana glanced at him and then away again. That irritated him too.

'Just about the fact that within a couple of days I'll be on the other side of the world, starting a whole new life.'

Caio felt something hard lodge in his chest. He should be cheering Ana on. He should be offering to make arrangements to rebook her flight. But that rudderless feeling was back. That feeling of needing to do something drastic.

For a man who had carved out a solitary path and made a huge success of it, he *should* be relishing this confirmation that she was okay with what had happened, and that she was happy to proceed with getting on with their separate lives.

He should be. But he wasn't.

He still wanted her.

The thought of her leaving, of not having her again, was…inconceivable. Caio was not used to not getting what he wanted. Yet here he was in this unique situation. Unprecedented. It had always been easy for him to say goodbye to a lover. But not this time.

He turned to face Ana. 'You don't have to go. You could stay.'

Ana went very still. Had she heard right? Or was her imagination playing tricks on her?

She forced herself to look at Caio. 'What did you say?'

He folded his arms over his chest. 'You could stay. You don't have to leave.'

'And do what, exactly?'

'Stay with me.'

Ana's heart thumped. 'We're divorced, Caio. In what capacity would I be staying with you?'

'As my lover.'

Ana hated the betraying bloom of hope deep inside when Caio wasn't really offering anything at all. Just a stay of execution. 'What do you think the gossips would make of that?'

'Since when did you care about society's opinion?'

That stung. Ana had to concede that, while she'd always disdained the world she'd been born into, she'd come to move within it in the past year with more ease than she'd like to admit. Sharing Caio's cynicism about many of the people in their world, she'd learnt not to take it so seriously. And she'd loved it that Caio's attitude to it all was to do his best to get the most out of people, to appeal to their very superficial sense of charity to extract as much money from them as possible and pass it on to worthy causes.

'You've spent a year in a marriage of convenience,' she pointed out. 'In order to shore up your reputation. And now you're willing to jeopardise it all? Just for sex?'

Caio's face flushed. 'This chemistry is… insane, Ana. I've never experienced anything like it. It's more than just sex.'

Ana's heart palpitated. *Exactly.* It was more than just sex. The stubborn bloom of hope was back. 'What exactly are you offering, Caio?'

'A chance to let this play out.'

A chance to let this play out. The bloom of hope faded again.

Ana folded her arms too. 'How long would you see this "playing out"?'

'A week…a month…who knows?'

The old hurt of abandonment and a sense of vulnerability made Ana say, 'What about a year? You managed to keep your hands off me for a whole year, Caio. Clearly I wasn't all that irresistible. Are you sure it's not just the island air going to your head?'

Caio's face tightened. 'I respected you, Ana. I didn't want to blur the lines.'

'So you don't respect the women you sleep with?'

Caio cursed. 'Of course I do. I didn't mean it like that.'

'But it's okay to sleep with me now because we're no longer married. Marriage really is a passion-killer for you, isn't it?'

Angry with herself for feeling torn by Caio's suggestion—tempted, but also devastated anew because it was more than obvious that he wasn't interested in more—Ana was galvanised to move. She picked up the strewn clothes from the beach and began to walk back up to the villa.

Caio was behind her. In the kitchen, Ana put the clothes into the washing machine and turned it on.

He said, 'So that's it, then? You're not interested?'

Ana stopped, but didn't turn to face him. *Not interested?* Her heart twisted. He had no idea. Every cell in her body clamoured at the sound of his voice. Her blood simmered. Between her legs she ached to feel him slide there again, thrusting so deep inside her she couldn't breathe. She knew she'd never experience that again. And it was heartbreaking.

She thought of something and went into the den. She found the picture and picked it up, then took it over to Caio. She held it out.

He said, 'What's this?'

Ana pushed it towards him. 'Look at it.'

He sighed, took it and looked. It was a photo of Luca Fonseca and his wife. She was heavily pregnant and sitting on his lap. They were both oblivious to the camera, looking at each other intently. His hand was on her bump. It was incredibly intimate and it had caught Ana's eye when Estella had been showing them around.

Ana knew she couldn't pretend that she was blasé about what had happened and about what she wanted.

She said, 'That's what I want, Caio. I want forever. In spite of everything I know, and in spite of everything I witnessed. My own mother walked away from me without looking back. I can't put myself through that again. Not for an affair.' She looked at Caio. 'You were right. We shouldn't have slept together. But I don't think you'll have any problem moving on. Now I'm going to pack and wait for the helicopter to come.'

CHAPTER TWENTY-ONE

FOR A LONG moment Caio just stood in the same spot, looking at the empty space Ana had left, holding the picture in his hand. He looked down at it again, feeling a little numb. At first he hadn't quite been able to make it out, almost as if it was in another language—as if he literally couldn't understand what he was seeing.

A couple. *Happiness. Intimacy. Family.* And something else he wasn't willing to name.

He couldn't think straight. Ana's words *'I don't think you'll have any problem moving on'* reverberated sickeningly in his head.

The was a massive pressure building up inside him, and he had to move or it would explode. He put the picture down on a table and went back outside, paced up and down.

He'd asked Ana to stay, to continue this affair…and she'd said no. Not something Caio was used to where women were concerned.

She'd said, *'I want forever.'* But not with him, evidently.

Not that he wanted forever. Ever since he'd been small and he and his brothers had been dominated and bullied by their father, and he'd seen his mother browbeaten and worse, he'd fostered an aversion to the notion of happy families and marriage. It didn't exist.

But when he'd believed that his mother was going to break away, prove him wrong, Caio had been surprised to find himself thinking that perhaps there could be some hope for a different existence. For choosing happiness.

That hope hadn't lived long. His mother had chosen to go back into a toxic situation, citing love as a reason. It had solidified Caio's beliefs that love and marriage spelled nothing but dysfunction.

Forever. What even *was* that? Ana knew as well as he did that it wasn't possible for people like them.

But then Caio's gut twisted. Maybe it was possible for her. Because she wasn't infected with his cynicism.

The picture of Luca Fonseca and his wife haunted him. He didn't know them well, so he couldn't attest to how authentic their union was, but he had a sick feeling that that picture was real, and if it was real, it upended a lot of Caio's assertions. Shifted the bedrock of his foundation. That he survived better alone. That love and marriage were toxic. That he didn't need anyone by his side.

You've had someone by your side for a year now, a little voice reminded him.

For the first few events it had felt strange, having someone by his side, someone he had to look out for. It had almost felt like an intrusion. But then…it hadn't.

He thought back to one of their first big events in Europe. London. A gala benefit dinner supporting a charity that helped disadvantaged young people to embrace technology and foster new talent in those who didn't have the advantages that someone like Caio had had.

Ana had gone to the restroom and the crowd had started to move into the main ballroom for dinner. There had been no sign of her. Irritation had prickled under Caio's skin. With hindsight, he could appreciate that his irritation hadn't just been down to the fact that he wasn't a solo operator any more…it had also been down to the fact that Ana had had her makeover that day, and the shock of her much sleeker and more elegant look had unsettled Caio in a way he hadn't liked at all.

As he'd waited for her in that hotel his irritation had mounted, and an insidious thought had entered Caio's head: *she's becoming a distraction.*

And then he'd seen her, and she'd been with a young man. Caio hadn't been prepared for the surge of something hot and volatile inside him. *Jealousy.* It had only been when they'd got closer that he'd realised the young man was actually a teenager and he looked incredibly nervous.

Ana, clearly putting the young boy at ease, had introduced him to Caio as a huge fan, and Caio had felt the volatility drain away. That evening something had shifted between them. He'd stopped feeling her presence was an intrusion. The distraction had remained, but he'd countered that by using their public appearances as an excuse to touch her. Reaching for her hand. Pulling her into his side.

He recognised now that he'd lived for those moments. He'd engineered them by accepting invitations to events that he wasn't even interested in. Yet he'd never admitted that to himself before now. He'd been too much of a coward to acknowledge his growing attraction. To admit that his wife of convenience was impacting on him in a profound way.

It had only been in the past month, since it had become harder and harder to remain immune to her, that he'd resisted touching her for fear of revealing himself.

Last night had blasted apart the illusion that he'd ever had any sense of control around Ana. He'd lost control a long time ago. What had happened between them in the last twenty-four hours had been a foregone conclusion for months. *Since the moment they'd met.*

Much to his shame and disgust, Caio was forced to admit now that Ana had had to be the one to initiate the seduction. Because he'd been in the grip of a desire so intense he couldn't have contemplated a rejection. So he'd let her come to him, and he'd resisted and resisted until he was sure that he was risking nothing. Except he'd risked everything.

Because for the first time in his life with a woman his emotions were at stake.

Caio stopped pacing as that sank in. As the full enormity of it gripped him.

At that moment he heard a distinctive noise in the distance, and before he could think about what he was doing he acted on an impulse too strong to ignore.

Ana frowned at the sky from her bedroom balcony. Where on earth was the helicopter going? It had been on a steady path towards the island, but suddenly it had banked to the right and now it was going back in the opposite direction.

Not that she'd noted the arrival of it with relief—more a sense of futility and loss. Annoyingly.

She also noticed that the security boats were gone. She was confused. She felt as if she should jump up and down and shout. Wave a bright-coloured shirt in the air. But they knew they were here…what were they doing?

Suddenly a suspicion formed. *Caio*. He was a man used to getting his own way.

Fuelled by a sense of anger, and far more betrayingly by excitement and hope, Ana left her things on the bed and went downstairs.

She found Caio in the kitchen, putting his phone back into his pocket. He turned around. Ana tried to ignore how her heart hitched.

'Why is the helicopter not landing?'

'I told them to go back to Rio and await further instructions. We're not done here, Ana.'

She'd been right. Anger at his high-handedness made her put her hands on her hips. 'Who do you think you are to make that decision on my behalf?'

Caio mirrored her, putting his hands on his hips. 'The man you chose…no, *begged* to be your first lover.'

Ana flushed with self-consciousness. 'I'm beginning to regret my decision.'

Caio took his hands down and moved closer. 'Are you really?'

Ana took a step back and put a hand out. 'Don't come near me, Caio.'

'Why? Because you can't think straight if I'm near you? Because you're afraid of what you'll do?'

Ana scooted around the kitchen island so that it was between them. She wasn't afraid of him; it was of herself she was terrified. He was right. Damn him.

She realised that Caio looked a little wild. As if his civilised veneer had been cracked open, revealing the elemental man she'd met last night.

'I would have thought you'd be delighted to return to work. To your life in Rio. Your usual lovers.'

'What life would that be, hmm? The life I led before? Where I cut myself off from my family and was dumped by women and friends who'd only accepted me for my family connections? And yet those were the first people who rushed back when I made my first million? Lovers who saw only the status I could offer them, and the expensive trinkets? Lovers who had no interest in who I really was? The life where I took my mother's name, casting aside hundreds of years of legacy, and worked twenty-four-seven to build up a business that needed a marriage of convenience to take it to the next level? A business that will die with me? Rendering everything I've done as futile?'

Surprised at his outburst, Ana said, 'It won't be futile. You've created innovations that will last forever.'

He waved a hand. 'They'll last until someone comes up with a better idea.' Then he continued, 'Or perhaps I should return to the life I've had for the past year, with a wife of convenience who turned out to be not as convenient as I expected?'

Ana swallowed. There was something dangerously exciting about this far more volatile Caio. 'You no longer have a wife. We're divorced, remember?'

Caio glanced down at her hand. 'You haven't stopped wearing your rings.'

Ana blinked and looked down to see the gold band and the very plain round cut diamond engagement ring that Caio had insisted she pick out for herself. She hadn't removed them.

She reached for them now, feeling exposed, but Caio said, 'Don't. Wait.'

CHAPTER TWENTY-TWO

ANA'S FINGERS WERE on the rings. She felt angry with Caio for delaying the inevitable. She pulled them off and put them on the island between them. 'Why would you not want me to take them off? We're no longer married.'

Caio ran his hands through his hair, clearly agitated. He looked at Ana. 'I thought I had it all mapped out—that I knew exactly what I wanted. You would be the perfect accompaniment, taking me to the next level, and in return you'd get your own freedom, and your brother's.' He started to pace back and forth. 'But then it wasn't just that I got used to you by my side. I began to *need* it. I told myself it wasn't that at all. That I just appreciated your opinion and the company you provided. I told myself I wasn't coming to depend on you...' He stopped pacing and looked at her. 'Do you remember when you had that tummy bug in Kuala Lumpur?'

Ana nodded. She'd seen that city through the triple-glazed glass of her bathroom and bedroom as she'd succumbed to a violent but thankfully short-lived stomach bug. It had meant, though, that she hadn't been able to attend one of the events with Caio.

'We'd only attended a few events by then, but when you weren't there...it bothered me. And it bothered me that it bothered me. I didn't like how you'd inserted yourself into my life so seamlessly. How I already felt a reflex to turn to you and see if you were okay. See your reaction to something. To *need* you by my side. I'd been coping fine for years. I didn't need anyone. But suddenly... I did.'

Ana swallowed. Not sure how to respond. She could remember how Caio had been a bit more distant than usual with her for a couple of weeks after that. She'd seen it as a judgement on her far too human frailties. But it hadn't been that at all.

She said, 'I didn't know. At every event I was just concentrating on not tripping over my own feet or saying something stupid.'

'I know. And you did yourself a disservice. You are a natural, warm person, and people gravitated to you because of that. You did more than help me enhance my business, Ana, you made *me* look like a better person.'

Ana's chest felt tight. 'You are a good person, Caio.'

He snorted. 'My focus has been singularly on myself—satisfying passing desires and building my own brand to the exclusion of thinking about anything or anyone else.'

'You thought about me,' Ana pointed out.

And he had. They could have lived very separate existences during their marriage, literally coming together only for public events. After all, that had been the agreement laid out in the marriage contract. But over the months they'd naturally gravitated towards spending more time together outside of those public appearances.

Caio had begun joining her for dinner in the evenings when nothing else was planned. Watching a documentary or a movie with her. And on days in foreign cities when he'd had to work, he'd always arranged for her to be taken on a tour with a private guide.

She said, almost to herself, 'There was that day in Paris…'

Caio looked at her. 'I think that was the start of it. I was finding it harder and harder to leave you to your own devices.'

They'd been in Paris and he'd arranged, as usual, for her to be taken to see the sights with a guide. He'd called her to see how she was getting on, and he'd sounded so wistful about her excursion that she'd joked, 'Why don't you join us?'

And he had. Ana had nearly fallen off her seat in the boat on the Seine when they'd made a stop to let him on. He'd dismissed the private guide and confided a little sheepishly that he'd been to Paris many times, but never seen the sights.

That day, they'd visited the Eiffel Tower, the Musée d'Orsay and the Louvre. And at one point, not thinking, Ana had taken Caio's hand—a moment borne out of excitement and appreciation for everything she was experiencing. She'd soon realised with a hot and cold flash of embarrassment what she'd done, and that it would serve no purpose, and she had pulled away saying, 'Sorry, I forgot for a moment...'

But Caio had held on and she'd looked up at him, her pulse suddenly going crazy. There'd been an arrested expression on his face, as if he too had forgotten, and then his grip had relaxed. The next time she'd pulled away he'd let her go.

That was when Ana had realised that she had to be more careful around him.

She felt dangerously close to exposing herself all over again now.

She shook her head. 'Caio...what's going on? Why are we still here?'

As if talking to himself, Caio said, 'You know, everything might still be okay if last night hadn't happened. You know why I resisted you for so long?'

Ana shook her head. Caio was moving slowly around the kitchen island. She was rooted to the spot.

'Because I knew that you were different. I knew that from the start. And I knew that if I gave in to the temptation to seduce you it would blow everything apart.'

'You didn't want me on our wedding night.'

His gaze narrowed on her face. The island no longer separated them. He was just a few feet away. 'When I saw you in that wedding dress—'

Ana ducked her head. 'That dress was awful. So unfashionable.'

Caio's bare feet came into her line of vision. His fingers tipped her face up. He shook his head. 'I've had fantasies about that dress. On our wedding night it was easy for me to pretend that the erotic charge I'd felt was some kind of aberration. But it didn't go away. It only grew stronger. Why do you think I threw myself into work so much? It was easier to deny my desire if I wasn't with you. But then it got harder to stay away.'

Ana pulled Caio's hand down and stepped back. Anger resurging—at the things he was saying, at the thought that the undercurrents she'd sensed between them hadn't all been in her head, a figment of her imagination.

'Why are you saying this now, Caio? What's the point?'

He looked grim. 'Because last night effectively blew the façade that everything was okay to pieces.'

'What's that supposed to mean?' Ana asked a little shakily.

'It means that this isn't over.'

Ana shook her head. 'Caio, I've already told you—'

'You've told me nothing. All you've done is point to a picture and say that you want *forever*.'

Ana gulped. 'I meant what I said.'

Caio's expression was stark. 'You're telling me you're able to walk away from what we started last night? That if I was to kiss you right now we wouldn't be making love right here within minutes?'

A wave of heat pulsed through her body.

'Are you telling me that was enough for you?' he demanded.

Anger at Caio's insistence on pushing Ana to expose herself utterly made her say angrily, 'No, it's not enough for me. But the problem is that it never will be, Caio. I knew from the moment we kissed that I was ruined. And I know after last night that the thought of another man touching me would make me sick.'

Tears stung Ana's eyes. She'd hoped and prayed that she could at least get off the island with her dignity intact. But now Caio would know everything and—

'Good.'

CHAPTER TWENTY-THREE

GOOD? THE WORD stopped Ana's whirling thoughts dead. She blinked back her emotion. Caio was looking smug. Anger turned to rage, because he was *loving* it that he'd ruined her for anyone else while he would just blithely go back to normal.

Ana lifted up an apple and threw it at him. It bounced off his shoulder.

He frowned. 'Hey, what's that for?'

She picked up another piece of fruit—a clementine. 'You arrogant, smug so-and-so.'

She fired the fruit at him, but he caught it.

She continued. 'You're so egotistical that you want to make sure I'll never think of another man again, while you can just take up where you left off and bask in the knowledge that I'll never forget you.'

She punctuated this by firing another piece of fruit in his direction. This time a plum. It missed by a mile. Caio started advancing on her again. She picked up a banana and held it threateningly.

He said, 'What are you going to do? Shoot me?'

Ana scowled and threw the banana down. She stopped moving back. 'What's your plan, Caio? To make me admit that I still want you? Well, I already have. To take me to bed again until you've got me out of your system? So you can get on with your life? Well, that's not going to happen. Call the helicopter back this minute. I'm ready to go.'

Ana had somehow backed herself into a corner. Caio was still advancing. She had nowhere to run or hide. She put up a hand to stop him, but he swatted it out of his way and scooped her up as if she weighed nothing, sat her on the island and wedged himself firmly between her legs.

Ana couldn't speak.

'That's better,' he said.

Ana opened her mouth, but he put a finger to her lips.

'Now, are you ready to listen to why I said *good*?'

Ana folded her arms. But it was impossible to ignore Caio. His face was inches from hers, and his lean hips were wedged between her thighs. She could smell him and, *Deus*, she wanted to touch him.

He was waiting for her to speak. She threw her arms up. 'Fine. I can't move anyway.'

His mouth twitched, but then he became serious. 'The reason I said *good* is because I feel exactly the same way. You have ruined me forever—but it is a beautiful ruin that I will take over and over again. The thought of ever touching another woman makes me feel panicky and nauseous all at once. From the moment we met, Ana, no other woman has interested me.'

Ana could feel the colour draining from her face. 'But I was wearing leggings...and a T-shirt.'

'And hiding behind your hair.'

Ana couldn't say another word. She just looked at Caio.

He went on. 'As for the thought of another man touching you—that makes me feel violent. And that scares me, because I do not want to resemble my father in any way.'

Ana touched Caio's face. 'You're nothing like your father.'

He turned his head and placed a kiss to the middle of the palm of her hand. She drew it back, still not entirely sure what was going on in spite of the way he was looking at her and the things he was saying. It was too huge. Too much of a sea-change.

As if sensing her trepidation, Caio said, 'You asked me about children, a family... asked me what was the point of my success there's no one to leave it all to. I've always rejected the idea of family because of my own toxic example, and I rejected the notion of legacy because that's what our families are built on—and look at what they've become... But I've come to realise that they might have started out with a very positive idea of legacy, but success and greed twisted them. You were right, Ana. What *is* the point of all this work—of extricating myself from my family and taking my mother's name—if I can't share it with someone else, or some day, hand it down to the next generation. They might not want it, but that's okay.'

Ana found her voice. 'They...? Who is *they*?'

'Our children.'

Suddenly it was too much. It was as if she was in some parallel dimension and Caio was articulating all her most secret fantasies. Except she'd never even allowed herself to indulge in this one.

She pushed at Caio until he moved back, and then slid down off the counter and escaped back to the other side of the island. She needed space. Air.

'What you're saying is… It's too much, Caio. I don't know if I believe you. Only yesterday you were saying that you don't believe in marriage or family. That that was why you wanted a marriage of convenience. Yet now…'

Caio looked at Ana. He saw the distrust in her eyes. On her face. And something else. A yearning. His insides twisted. It was all so clear to him now, but not to her, and he had a sickening sense that no matter what he said she wouldn't believe him. And he couldn't really blame her. After all, he'd done a spectacular job for the last few months—and hours—of living in a state of denial.

He ran a hand through his hair. 'Look, Ana, I know this is hard to grasp, but everything I'm saying has been here…' he touched his chest '…building up.' He cursed silently. It sounded weak to his own ears.

She lifted her chin. 'Last night, *I* seduced *you*. I'll never know if you would have seduced me.'

The hum of desire inside Caio refuted that. 'I was a coward. I wanted you too much to risk trying to seduce you and you rejecting me.'

Ana's eyes widened. '*You* were scared of

me rejecting *you*.' Her tone was flat. She folded her arms. 'What if last night hadn't happened?'

'I think I would have lasted about a week before following you to Amsterdam and seducing you into coming back to Rio.'

He knew that now. The absence of Ana would have thrown everything into sharp relief.

He said, 'All last night did was accelerate the process.'

Ana shook her head. 'I don't believe you.'

Caio seized on something he'd forgotten about. 'So why did I book to go to a conference in Dublin in ten days' time? A conference that has asked me to deliver the keynote speech every year for the past five years, and this year I said yes.'

Ana looked doubtful.

Caio's guts clenched. 'In case it's not obvious by now… I love you, Ana. And, believe me, no one is more surprised than me that I'm saying those words. But, quite simply, the thought of you leaving, of you being out in the world without me, is terrifying. Why do you think that gang targeted us? They'd been following us for months…they saw something that we weren't even ready to admit to ourselves. They knew I'd do whatever it took to get you back.'

Ana looked at him for a long moment. Her face was pale. Eyes huge. Eventually she said, 'You see, the thing is, Caio, that I've loved you for some time now. In spite of my best instincts and my attempts to stop myself from falling for you because I knew you were all wrong for me. And it wasn't as if you gave me any encouragement. But I fell for you anyway. Maybe you believe you love me for now, after last night...but you're the one who warned me about confusing sex with emotion, Caio. Maybe you need to take your own advice.'

She turned and walked out of the villa, but not before he'd seen the glint of emotion in her eyes.

Not for the first time in twenty-four hours, Caio felt helpless. A hollow ache spread through him. A sense of futility. His dogged cynicism and strong sense of self-preservation mocked him mercilessly. He'd not only convinced himself that he was above such mortal concerns as love and connection...he'd convinced Ana too.

CHAPTER TWENTY-FOUR

ANA STOOD ON the beach looking out to sea. Funny how she kept gravitating to this place. *Caio had told her he loved her.* How she'd managed to walk away from him after he'd said that, she wasn't sure. Her legs still felt like jelly. But she couldn't afford to believe him. The risk was too huge. If her own mother could turn her back on her and walk away, then a man who'd briefly confused passion and sex with emotion could do far worse.

And it would be infinitely more painful this time.

She'd never heal from it and she'd become as cynical and self-protective as him.

That thought made her stop.

It made her think about a young boy growing up—superfluous to requirements, all but ignored by his father and brothers, with a brittle mother living in the shadow of her domineering husband.

She thought of Caio watching that. Absorbing it. Seeing the moment when his mother had decided to take a chance and fight for her own survival only to go back, proving to Caio that any attempt to find one's own emotional happiness was just not worth it. And then his experience at the hands of his first lover.

She knew where his bone-deep cynicism came from. That was why she couldn't trust that he'd let it go so quickly. No matter how much she wanted to.

The sun was rising into the sky. It was almost exactly twenty-four hours since they'd signed the papers in Rio.

She would have to be strong. She would have to tell Caio that—

She heard a noise behind her and tensed. She started to turn around, but Caio said, 'Don't turn around. Not yet.'

Ana stayed where she was.

For a long moment Caio said nothing, and then, 'I know what you're thinking. That it's too much too soon. That you can't trust that I mean what I say.'

Ana was glad that she was facing away from Caio, that he couldn't see her expression.

'The truth is that this isn't something that's just happened. It started when we first met, Ana. On our wedding day when you walked down the aisle in that dress. And when you said to me that you were sorry for being late.' He continued, 'I know you hated that dress, and I know you felt uncomfortable and unfashionable. But *I* found that dress erotic. I had fantasies about the wedding night we never got to share. Fantasies about stripping that dress off you and baring your body to my gaze.'

He made a small sound—a curt, laughing noise.

'I put those thoughts down to some weird reaction to getting married. But every day you were sinking deeper and deeper into my head and my blood. You fascinated me. Your habits. Your interests. I'd never spent so much time with a woman in a platonic setting. But what I was feeling for you wasn't platonic. And yet... you became my friend too, Ana. The first real friend I ever had. I always shut everyone out. Rejected them before they could reject me. And I know you can appreciate that because you did it too. Except you were lucky—you had Francisco.

'You crept under my skin in such a way that it took me until our divorce, with the prospect of you walking away, for me to fully acknowledge just how integral you'd become to my life. To me. And it took last night and blowing the world to pieces for me to realise that what I feel for you goes so much deeper than transient desire. There's nothing transient about how you make me feel, Ana.'

Ana only realised she was holding her breath when her body forced her to take a huge shuddering breath in, making her lightheaded.

Caio said, 'I know what your mother's rejection did to you. I can't even imagine that pain. And yet you're brave, because you're not letting it define you. You know you want more, and you won't rest until you find it. You're infinitely braver than me. I know you, Ana. I know every part of you. I love how you came out of your shell and blossomed into the beautiful woman you are. I love how you've realised that you can navigate our world with more skill and ease than you'd like to admit because otherwise it means that somehow *they've* won. But they haven't won. You've won. Because you navigate society with humanity and compassion—and that's the difference. I love experiencing the world with you. And I can't keep pretending that I don't want forever too. I was done with my emotionally empty existence a long time before I acknowledged it. I'm tired of the cynicism and jadedness. I want more. Joy. Happiness. *You*. Forever.'

Ana's vision was blurry. With every word Caio dismantled the last of her defences. Even if it turned out that this was all an elaborate play to keep her in his bed just for as long as he wanted her then she knew she couldn't refuse. He'd broken her.

'You can turn around now.'

Wiping her eyes, Ana slowly turned around—but Caio wasn't there. It took her a second to realise he was kneeling down, and she had to adjust her eyeline.

She frowned. 'Caio…?'

He was looking incredibly nervous, and was holding her wedding and engagement rings in the palm of his hand. Ana's heart skipped.

'Ana Diaz, will you marry me? For real this time? And not just for a year, but until death us do part. Because anything less won't do for me.'

Ana's legs went from jelly to water. She collapsed onto her knees in front of Caio. He reached for her and she went into his arms in the same breath, the two of them falling back onto the sand, his body cushioning hers, a hard-muscled cushion.

She looked down at him. 'Caio…'

She realised she had a torrent of words to

say—voicing all her doubts and insecurities and fears. The enduring vision of her mother walking away. Her father's indifference. Feeling insecure. Vulnerable. But now those things faded away. She felt strong. Invincible. No matter what.

All the words melted on her tongue. Except for one. *'Yes.'*

His eyes widened. His arms tightened around her. 'Ana...?'

She smiled at his shock. At his very uncharacteristic insecurity. 'Yes, Caio. *Yes.* Let's get married again—for real this time.'

Suddenly Ana was on her back on the sand and Caio was hovering over her, looking intense. 'Ana, I... You...'

She took pity on him and put a finger to his mouth. 'Just kiss me, Caio. We have a lot of catching up to do.'

His gaze went to her mouth, hungry. He lowered his head, Ana wrapped her arms around his neck, and they kissed for a long time, until the tide reached their feet.

Before they left the beach Ana held out her hand and Caio put the rings back onto her finger. The enormity of what had happened here within twenty-four hours caught at her heart. But Caio was right. It hadn't been twenty-four hours—it had been happening for a year.

They walked back into the villa barefoot, clothes dishevelled, hand in hand. At the doorway Ana said, 'What about the helicopter?'

Caio pulled her close. 'It's on standby for whenever we need it. There's no rush, is there?'

Ana looped her arms around his neck and pressed close, revelling in the evidence of his desire for her. 'No rush at all. Take me to bed, Caio.'

Caio scooped Ana into his arms and carried her through the villa to the bedroom. They made love and whispered vows and promises, told each other of all the things they'd keep secret for so long.

And finally, about a week later, when the food ran out, they called for the helicopter to come and get them.

A month later, Civil Register Office, Rio de Janeiro

Ana stood outside the main doors of the register office. She was nervous. Her brother Francisco, whom Caio had flown home for today, took her hands.

'Ana, *why* are you wearing that hideous dress again?'

Ana giggled and hiccuped at the same

time, emotion high in her chest. 'It's a private thing.'

Her brother shook his head and put her arm in his. 'Straight people are so weird,' he muttered.

Ana was wearing her wedding dress again. On strict instructions from her fiancé, who had told her in forensic detail how he wanted to dispense with it later.

A flash of gold and yellow caught her eye and she looked down to see the new engagement ring he'd surprised her with when they'd eventually returned to Rio from the island. A square yellow diamond in a gold setting.

He had her gold wedding band, and she had his.

Her hair was up in a loose knot. She wore small diamond earrings. Minimal make-up. Carried a small posy of seasonal flowers.

In the seconds before the doors opened Ana had a flashback to her first wedding day, when she'd stood outside the church doors with her father. She'd never really admitted it to herself before now, but she'd felt an incredible sense of loss that day. The loss of a dream she'd harboured so deeply that she'd been too afraid to acknowledge it. A dream of walking down the aisle towards someone she loved. Who loved her. Towards a life that she'd never experienced but which she still hoped existed.

She hadn't seen Caio in twenty-four hours, because he'd had a business meeting in Sao Paulo and they'd both wanted to observe the tradition of not seeing each other before the wedding.

Except last night Ana had been beset by doubts and fears. She knew how long twenty-four hours could be. After all, their lives had changed in twenty-four hours on that island. What if all it took for Caio to realise he was making a huge mistake was another twenty-four hours?

She hated herself for feeling so insecure.

The doors to the register office suddenly opened and Francisco squeezed her hand. The second Ana's eyes met Caio's all her doubts and fears melted into a pool of heat. Love swelled in her chest, making it tight.

His molten gaze held hers until she reached him, and then he took her hand, acknowledged Francisco briefly, before pulling Ana into his side. Oblivious to the registrar, he said, 'I missed you... I was afraid—'

Ana felt tears prick her eyes. 'I know...me too.'

Caio kissed Ana until an insistent coughing broke through the intense bubble they were in.

They came up for air and the registrar began proceedings.

Afterwards, when the rabid press had got their fill of pictures of Caio and Ana's remarriage, and after they'd danced and drunk wine and celebrated, Caio carried a deliciously dishevelled Ana into the bedroom in their apartment.

He put her down on her feet by the bed and stood back. Ana devoured him with her eyes. His white shirt, open at the top. Black trousers. Stubble lining his jaw.

His gaze devoured her right back. Travelling down over her breasts to her waist and hips. To her bare feet.

Ana squirmed slightly. She wanted to be out of the dress so they were skin on skin… but Caio had other ideas.

He came towards her and shook his head. 'I've been waiting for a long time for this moment.'

He turned her around and started undoing the small buttons at the back of the dress. Ana shivered slightly as the cool air touched her skin, followed by Caio's mouth and tongue.

Already breathless, she said plaintively, 'I really don't mind if you just want to rip it off…'

Caio put his hands on her waist and pressed

a kiss to the side of her neck. 'Oh, no, meu amor, there will be no ripping…'

His hands came up to cup her breasts under the lacy material. Ana squirmed, pushing her bottom against him. But Caio showed more restraint than her and, as promised, it was a long and slow and deliciously torturous process.

When the dress was finally dispensed with, and lying in a pool of silk and lace on the floor, Ana was feverish with lust.

Caio seated himself between her legs and entwined his fingers with hers, holding her hands above her head. He thrust deep into her body and she arched against him. She'd never felt so full, so impaled… Their eyes met and Caio started to move, never taking his eyes off hers.

Words trembled on her lips.

Caio pressed a kiss to her mouth and said huskily, 'I know, love. Me too. Forever.'

Pleasure broke Ana into a million pieces, with Caio following just seconds later. He tucked her into his body and she pressed a kiss to his shoulder. She whispered an echo of love against his skin. 'Forever.'

EPILOGUE

Five years later

'ANA DIAZ SALAZAR.'

Everyone clapped as Ana got up from her seat and walked to the podium in her black gown and cap, the golden tassel swinging beside her beaming face. Her hair was glossy and longer now, falling below her shoulders in loose waves.

She wore a cream floaty wrap dress underneath the gown, and high heels. The only jewellery she wore was a pair of diamond drop earrings, her wedding ring and engagement ring. Someone indiscreet behind Caio noted waspily that for a billionaire's wife she wasn't exactly blingy, but she was very pretty.

Caio turned around to the gossipers, smiled benevolently, and said, 'She's the most beautiful woman in the world. She doesn't need adornment.'

The two women nearly fell off their chairs.

Caio turned back to see Ana shaking the hand of the president of the university and accepting her first class honours degree. She smiled for the cameras. And then the moment Caio had hoped they would avoid happened, when their three-year-old daughter Luna woke up abruptly and spotted Ana on the stage.

'Look! Mama!'

Ana saw them and Caio smiled at her minute eye-roll. His heart expanded with love and pride as she re-joined her fellow classmates and they waited for the rest of the ceremony to finish.

After Ana had said emotional goodbyes to friends and professors, and had handed back her ceremonial gown and cap, she went looking for Caio and Luna. He'd taken their daughter outside in case she was too noisy.

She spotted them before they saw her. They were down by the river which ran along the bottom of a beautiful landscaped lawn. The air was laden with the scent of flowers and cut grass. Students posed with families and smiled. Other students, not graduating, sat on the grass and ate lunch, or discussed lectures.

Ana's eyes went back to Caio and Luna. Two dark heads together as he held her safely while she squealed and pointed at the ducks. Ana's hand went to her chest for a minute, to try and contain her emotion as the full impact of the scene she was looking at sank in.

Caio had done this. Given her a chance to pursue her dream. To give her wings. But to keep her rooted at the same time—rooted in his unconditional love and security.

This was what she'd always dreamt of, and it was so much more than she'd ever believed might be possible. And there was more. She put a hand to her belly and the growing bump under her dress. She was almost five months pregnant with their second child. The light flutters of the last couple of weeks were getting stronger daily.

As if sensing her regard, Caio turned his head and found her unerringly. As he always did. He stood up, taking Luna into his arms, and Ana walked down towards them and straight into his arms. *Home.*

He drew her in for a kiss, and Ana relished his scent and the steely strength of his body. She could feel the inevitable spark of desire, still there, as strong as ever.

Reading her mind, Caio smirked at her. 'Wait till I get you home, Mrs Salazar.'

She winked at him. 'Promises, promises...'

Luna launched herself at Ana, wrapping

her small arms around her neck, and Ana buried her face in Luna's neck, making her laugh when she nuzzled her. Their daughter had her father's dark golden eyes and dark hair, and it took all their collective wits to keep up with her.

Caio said softly, 'I'm so proud of you.'

Ana's vision blurred a little. 'I'm proud of me too.'

Her husband took her hand and kissed it. 'You should be—you've worked hard.'

Caio took Luna back into his arms and held Ana's hand as he led her through the leafy and idyllic grounds of the university to the waiting car that would take them back to the townhouse he'd bought in Mayfair when he'd suggested moving to London, so that Ana could pursue her dream of studying and getting a degree in an English university.

For the last four years Caio had based his head office in London and had commuted to far flung places only when absolutely necessary. And only when Ana's schedule had allowed her to travel with him.

They hadn't planned on Ana getting pregnant so soon, but inevitably their insane chemistry had led to increasingly lax efforts to protect her against pregnancy—*et voilà*, Luna.

Luna had been very obliging—her due date

had been after Ana's first-year exams. And Caio had taken to fatherhood like a duck to water, regularly taking Luna to work in a papoose, and setting up a creche in his building to facilitate employees with families.

Ana would have been jealous of their bond if it didn't make her so happy that their daughter would experience the kind of father/daughter relationship she and her brother had never had. Nor Caio.

But within the next few weeks they were moving back to Rio, so that Caio could refocus his energies on South America, now that he was firmly established in Europe and North America. Ana had ambitions to set up a publishing company, specialising in nurturing new voices in fiction from all over the world. And, they had an island waiting for them to spend some serious family downtime together.

Caio had surprised Ana on the first anniversary of their second wedding, when he'd taken her back to the island for a holiday and presented her with a piece of paper.

She'd unfolded it, but hadn't understood what she was looking at for a long moment. Eventually she'd choked out, 'You've bought the island from Luca Fonseca? For…*me*?'

Caio had nodded. 'I've had it renamed Ilha Ana. It's yours.'

Ana hadn't been able to speak for a long moment, and then she'd launched herself at Caio. She was pretty sure that what had happened next had resulted in their daughter, born approximately nine months later.

Later that evening, after the graduation, Caio surprised Ana with a celebratory dinner, together with her brother Francisco and his new partner, in one of London's most exclusive restaurants with views over the sparkling city.

When they'd returned to the house and checked on Luna—flat on her back, snoring gently—they went to their own bedroom and Ana, still emotional, turned to Caio.

'Thank you—not just for this evening, but for...everything. The last few years... No one has ever believed in me like you do. I would never have had the nerve to do it all without you.'

Caio tipped Ana's chin up. He looked serious. 'Yes, you would. You're one of the bravest people I know. This was all *you*. I followed you here, my love, and I'd follow you to the ends of the earth.'

Ana shook her head, protesting, but before she could say another word Caio was taking something out of his pocket. A small square velvet box. Ridiculously, he looked nervous.

'Caio…?'

He opened the box to reveal a simple gold ring studded with tiny diamonds. He said, 'It's an eternity ring. Because I will love you and want you for all eternity, Ana Diaz Salazar. Every day I marvel that I kept my distance from you for that whole year, but that was because I knew deep down that the minute I touched you I'd be yours. It took twenty-four hours for me to fall so deep and so hard that my life changed forever. You taught me that being cynical was a very weak protection and that love exists.'

Ana's eyes stung with emotion.

Caio took the ring out of the box, but before he put it on Ana's finger he showed her the inscription on the inside. It said, in beautifully delicate calligraphy, *One Night is Forever. Ana & Caio.* There was a date too—the date they'd spent that first night on the island. The night they'd been reborn.

Ana said in a choked voice, 'It's beautiful.'

Caio slipped it onto her finger and Ana wound her arms around his neck, pressing close, her curves melting against his hardness.

'I love you, Caio, and I want to spend my one night with you every night. Forever.'

He smiled. 'Forever it is.'

That night melted into many more days and

nights, filled with their growing family and a love that only grew more rooted. Their names were added to the urban legend of a very few others that were spoken about in hushed, disbelieving tones—because they were the real thing. Truly in love and happy.

But, wait, that couldn't possibly exist... could it?

* * * * *

If you loved the drama in
Their One-Night Rio Reunion
you're sure to love these other stories
by Abby Green!

The Maid's Best Kept Secret
The Innocent Behind the Scandal
Bride Behind the Desert Veil
The Flaw in His Red-Hot Revenge
Bound by Her Shocking Secret

Available now!